THE TRAGEDY OF MACBETH

Globe Book Company
A Division of Simon & Schuster
Englewood Cliffs, New Jersey

AN ADAPTED CLASSIC

THE TRAGEDY OF MACBETH

WILLIAM SHAKESPEARE

 GLOBE BOOK COMPANY
A Division of Simon & Schuster
Englewood Cliffs, New Jersey

Cover design: Marek Antoniak
Cover illustration: John Canizzo
Interior photos: Museum of Modern Art/Film Stills Archive

ISBN: 0-83590-015-0

Printed in the United States of America.
10   9   8   7   6   5   4   3   2   1

Globe Book Company
A Division of Simon & Schuster
Englewood Cliffs, New Jersey

ABOUT THE AUTHOR

William Shakespeare was born in Stratford-on-Avon, England, in 1564. It is believed that he attended school there, although there are no records to prove it. Records do show that he married and had children, and that by 1592 he was working as an actor and playwright in London.

During his years in London, Shakespeare belonged to an organization that put on plays. He was one of the company's actors, although apparently not a great star as an actor. Much more important were the plays, 37 in all, that he wrote for the company. In his time, the success of these plays made him a wealthy man.

About 1612, Shakespeare retired from the theater and returned to Stratford. He died there in 1616. After his death, his friends and admirers gathered copies of all his plays and had them published in one volume, the so-called First Folio of 1623. Today these plays stand as the greatest body of writing by one man in the English language, and perhaps in any language.

ADAPTOR'S NOTE

In preparing this edition of Macbeth all of Shakespeare's original language has been kept. Some lines have been cut to make the plot clearer and easier to follow. Extensive footnotes, summaries, and prereading material have been included to make Shakespeare's vocabulary an story accessible to the modern reader.

INTRODUCTION

Macbeth is a tragedy in the classical sense, that is, as the ancient Greeks understood the word *tragedy.* The central character of the play, Macbeth, is a tragic hero. The tragic hero is a man of high social standing and admirable personal qualities who has a "tragic flaw." In Macbeth's case, it is ambition. This quality is not in itself evil, but excessive ambition proves to be Macbeth's undoing.

At the beginning of the play, we see Macbeth as brave, honest and loyal. By the end, his ambition has driven him to commit one horrible act after another until he cannot stop. The members of the audience are frightened by these acts. Yet, they can also feel pity for Macbeth because they recognize in him those same human traits that they share. Finally, Macbeth's murders and violence turn him into a man with no emotions. It is not hard to think of modern examples of this kind of personal descent into degradation.

Shakespeare knew well the needs and feelings that human beings will always have. These timeless truths, along with his ability to create stories that hold the audience's attention, his believable characters, and his unequaled use of the English language, have assured the popularity of this play through the centuries.

Before experiencing *Macbeth,* either by reading it or seeing a production of it, some information about the circumstances of the first performance will help. The first public performance of *Macbeth* probably took place at the Globe Theatre in London.

The Globe Theatre, built in 1599, was an octagonal building with an open yard in the center, where people could stand for performances for the price of a penny. The rows of seats were against the walls of the building and were covered by a thatched roof. The stage was a wooden rectangular platform that extended into the yard.

Outdoor scenes were played on this platform, which had trapdoors that enabled actors playing ghosts or witches to appear and disappear. Behind the main stage was an inner stage with two levels that was used for indoor scenes. The upper level was used for bedroom or balcony scenes. On top of the upper level was a room called "the heavens" where stagehands could produce thunder and other sound effects.

Although the actors wore costumes, there was little or no scenery. When you read *Macbeth*, notice that the characters are always describing their surroundings and the weather. Shakespeare's language and his audiences' imaginations provided the scenery. This lack of realistic scenery also explains the rapid changes of place from scene to scene. With no scenery to move, the actors could be on a mountaintop one moment and in a castle room the next. These quick scene changes make Shakespeare's plays somewhat like motion pictures, but in the plays the information is provided by language, not visual images. Actors had to have good voices and excellent pronunciation. Not surprisingly, audiences of Shakespeare's time spoke of "hearing" plays rather than "seeing" them.

Performances at the Globe Theater took place in the afternoon in good weather, and the stage was lit by daylight. Shakespeare probably gave the witches the first scene in *Macbeth* to get the audience's attention right away. Many people believed in witches in Shakespeare's time, and the three that he created in *Macbeth* are the most famous in literature. It is doubtful that Shakespeare himself believed in witches, but he knew that they could be powerful characters on stage.

In fact, the problem of literal truth in his stageworks was not one that bothered Shakespeare. Playwrights of the time were more interested in what worked on stage, or what pleased an audience, than in historical accuracy. The real King Macbeth ruled Scotland from 1040 to 1057 A.D., and he got to the throne by killing King Duncan. Many of the other characters in the play and most of the action were made up by Shakespeare.

Macbeth is set in eleventh-century Scotland because it was written to please King James I of England, who was on the throne in 1606. James was a member of the Stuart family. The Stuarts had been rulers of Scotland for several centuries. James believed that Banquo, one of the most appealing and honorable characters in the play, had been the ancestor of the first of the Stuart kings.

The first performance of *Macbeth* may have been given privately at court, but it was clearly written with the larger audience of the Globe Theatre in mind. The rich language of Shakespeare's plays was not intended for the upper classes alone. His vocabulary was familiar and easily understood by most theatergoers of the time. Reading and understanding these plays is more of a challenge today, but the rewards of knowing and experiencing a play like *Macbeth* are worth the effort.

CONTENTS

DRAMATIS PERSONAE

DUNCAN, *King of Scotland*
MALCOLM, ⎤
DONALBAIN, ⎦ *his sons*

MACBETH, *Thane of Glamis, later of Cawdor,*
  later King of Scotland
LADY MACBETH

BANQUO, a thane of Scotland
FLEANCE, his son
MACDUFF, Thane of Fife
LADY MACDUFF
SON of Macduff and Lady Macduff

LENNOX, ⎤
ROSS, ⎥
MENTEITH, ⎥ *thanes and noblemen of Scotland*
ANGUS, ⎥
CAITHNESS, ⎦

SIWARD, *Earl of Northumberland*
YOUNG SIWARD, *his son*
SEYTON, *an officer attending Macbeth*
Another LORD
ENGLISH DOCTOR
SCOTTISH DOCTOR
GENTLEWOMAN *attending Lady Macbeth*
CAPTAIN *serving Duncan*
PORTER
OLD MAN
Three MURDERERS *of Banquo*

FIRST MURDERER *at Macduff's castle*
MESSENGER *to Lady Macbeth*
MESSENGER *to Lady Macduff*
SERVANT *to Macbeth*
SERVANT *to Lady Macbeth*
Three WITCHES *or* WEIRD SISTERS
HECATE
Three APPARITIONS

Lords, Gentlemen, Officers, Soldiers, Murderers, and Attendants

SCENE: *Scotland; England*

Before You Read Act I, Scene 1

The first scene of Macbeth is only thirteen lines long, but there is much information here about what will happen in the play. The stage directions say the scene is in an open place. What kind of open space do you imagine this would be? What kind of mood is Shakespeare creating in this scene? (Pay attention to the closing lines that the witches speak in this scene.) Notice that these three witches have a talent, or ability, that not all witches have.

ACT I. Scene 1.

Location: An open place.

[*Thunder and lightning.* Enter three WITCHES]

FIRST WITCH.
When shall we three meet again?
In thunder, lightning, or in rain? [1]

SECOND WITCH.
When the hurlyburly's done, [2]
When the battle's lost and won.

THIRD WITCH.
That will be ere the set of sun.

FIRST WITCH.
Where the place?

SECOND WITCH.
                              Upon the heath.[3]

THIRD WITCH.
There to meet with Macbeth.

FIRST WITCH.
I come, Grimalkin! [4]

---

1. **In thunder ... rain.** (People believed that witches could create storms about them.)
2. **hurlyburly.** noisy confusion (of battle)
3. **heath.** open wasteland
4. **Graymalkin.** gray cat (name of the witch's helper)

SECOND WITCH.
　Paddock calls. [5]

THIRD WITCH.

　　　　　Anon. [6]

ALL.
　Fair is foul, and foul is fair. [7]
　Hover through the fog and filthy air.

　　　　　　　　　　　　　　[Exit]

---

5. **Paddock.** toad; also a helper
6. **Anon.** at once, right away
7. **Fair is foul ... fair.** Good is evil, and evil is good.

Synopsis of Act I, Scene 1

Three witches appear in an open place. There is thunder and lightning, which helps to establish a frightening, evil mood. The three discuss a future meeting. The First Witch asks when the next meeting will be, and the Second Witch replies that they will meet when the battle is over. The Third Witch already knows when this will be, before sunset. The First Witch asks where. On the heath, replies the Third. They are going to meet Macbeth. It is clear that these witches know what will happen in the future. The witches depart, calling to their helpers, a gray cat and a toad. As they leave they all say good is evil and evil is good. The witches are interested in Macbeth for some evil reason.

Before You Read Act I, Scene 2

In this scene we first hear of the play's hero, Macbeth, but we do not actually see him. There is a fierce battle being fought near the military camp where this scene takes place. Duncan, King of Scotland, gets news of the the battle from a wounded captain, who has just come from the battlefield. He describes Macbeth's actions in the battle. What impression do we get from this description? How does King Duncan react to it? There is also news of another man who has behaved differently from Macbeth. What happens to him? Notice the first words in the scene. ("What bloody man is that?") The mention of blood sets the tone of this scene (and gives an early hint of what comes later in the play).

ACT I. Scene 2.

Location: A camp near Forres, a town in northeast Scotland.

[*Alarum within. Enter* KING (DUNCAN), [1] MALCOLM, DONALBAIN, LENNOX, *with attendants, meeting a bleeding* CAPTAIN.]

DUNCAN.
   What bloody man is that? He can report,
   As seemeth by his plight, of the revolt
   The newest state.

MALCOLM.
                        This is the sergeant [2]
   Who like a good and hardy soldier fought
   'Gainst my captivity. Hail, brave friend!
   Say to the King the knowledge of the broil [3]
   As thou didst leave it.

CAPTAIN.
                        Doubtful it stood,
   As two spent swimmers that do cling together
   And choke their art. The merciless Macdonwald— [4]
   Worthy to be a rebel, for to that [5]
   The multiplying villanies of nature [6]

---

1. **Alarum within.** trumpet call offstage
2. **sergeant.** officer
3. **broil.** battle
4. **choke their art.** prevent each other from swimming
5. **to that.** to that end
6. **multiplying ... him.** growing number of wicked rebels swarm about him like vermin

Do swarm upon him —from the Western Isles [7]
Of kerns and gallowglasses is supplied; [8]
And Fortune, on his damnèd quarrel smiling, [9]
Showed like a rebel's whore. But all's too weak; [10]
For brave Macbeth —well he deserves that name— [11]
Disdaining Fortune, with his brandished steel,
Which smoked with bloody execution,
Like valor's minion carved out his passage [12]
Till he faced the slave, [13]
Which ne'er shook hands nor bade farewell to him [14]
Till he unseamed him from the nave to the chops, [15]
And fixed his head upon our battlements.

DUNCAN.
O valiant cousin, worthy gentleman! [16]

CAPTAIN.
As when the sun 'gins his reflection [17]
Shipwrecking storms and direful thunders break, [18]
So from that spring whence comfort seemed to come

---

7. **Western Isles.** the Hebrides (off Scotland)
8. **Of kerns.** with light-armed Irish foot soldiers.
   gallowglasses. men on horses with axes
9. **quarrel.** cause
10. **Showed ... whore.** falsely appeared to favor Macdonwald
11. **name.** "brave"
12. **minion.** favorite
13. **slave.** Macdonwald
14. **Which.** who (referring to Macbeth). **ne'er ... to him.**
   acted   without politeness
15. **unseamed ... chops.** split him open from the navel to the
   jaws
16. **cousin.** kinsman
17. **As whence.** just as from the place where.   **'gins his**
   reflection. rises
18. **break.** come from

Discomfort swells. Mark, King of Scotland, mark. [19]
No sooner justice had, with valor armed,
Compelled this skipping kerns to trust their heels [20]
But the Norweyan lord, surveying vantage [21]
With furbished arms and new supplies of men,
Began a fresh assault.

DUNCAN.
Dismayed not this our captains, Macbeth and
Banquo?

CAPTAIN.
Yes, as sparrows eagles, or the hare the lion.
If I say sooth, I must report they were [22]
As cannons overcharged with double cracks, [23]
So they doubly redoubled strokes upon the foe.
Except they meant to bathe in reeking wounds [24]
Or memorize another Golgotha, [25]
I cannot tell.
But I am faint. My gashes cry for help.

DUNCAN.
So well thy words become thee as thy wounds;
They smack of honor both. —Go get him surgeons.
                    [*Exit* CAPTAIN, *attended*]

[*Enter* ROSS *and* ANGUS]

Who comes here?

19. **swells.** wells up
20. **skipping.** quick
21. **Norweyan lord.** King of Norway.
    surveying vantage. seeing an opportunity
22. **sooth.** truth
23. **cracks.** explosives
24. **Except.** unless
25. **memorize ... Golgotha.** make the place as memorable for
    slaughter as Golgotha, the place where Christ was crucified

MALCOLM.
> The worthy Thane of Ross. [26]

LENNOX.
> What a haste looks through his eyes!
> So should he look that seems to speak things
>   strange. [27]

ROSS.
> God save the King!

DUNCAN.
> Whence cam'st thou, worthy thane?

ROSS.
> From Fife, great King,
> Where the Norweyan banners flout the sky [28]
> And fan our people cold. [29]
> Norway himself, with terrible numbers, [30]
> Assisted by that most disloyal traitor,
> The Thane of Cawdor, began a dismal conflict, [31]
> Till that Bellona's bridegroom, lapped in proof, [32]
> Confronted him with self-comparisons, [33]
> Point against point, rebellious arm 'gainst arm,
> Curbing his lavish spirit; and to conclude, [34]
> The victory fell on us.

---

26. **Thane.** a Scottish title of nobility
27. **seems to.** seems about to
28. **flout.** mock
29. **fan ... cold.** fan cold fear into our troops
30. **Norway.** the King of Norway
31. **dismal.** threatening
32. **Bellona's ... proof.** Macbeth is called the mate of Bellona, the Roman goddess of war, clad in well-tested armor.
33. **him.** the King of Norway. **self-comparisons.** terms of peace
34. **lavish.** insolent

DUNCAN.

Great happiness!

ROSS.
That now
Sweno, the Norways' king, craves composition; [35]
Nor would we deign him burial of his men
Till he disbursèd at Saint Colme's Inch [36]
Ten thousand dollars to our general use. [37]

DUNCAN.
No more that Thane of Cawdor shall deceive
Our bosom interest. Go pronounce his present
    death, [38]
And with his former title great Macbeth.

ROSS.
I'll see it done.

DUNCAN.
What he hath lost noble Macbeth hath won.

[*Exit*]

---

35. Norways'. Norwegians'. **composition.** terms of peace
36. Saint Colme's Inch. island near Edinburgh, Scotland
37. dollars. Spanish or Dutch coins
38. Our. the royal "we". **our bosom interest.** my heart's
    trust. **present.** immediate

Synopsis of Act I, Scene 2

The battle the witches mentioned is being waged in northeast Scotland between King Duncan of Scotland and his army and the army of Macdonwald, an Irish rebel. In a military camp near the town of Forres, we first meet King Duncan, his sons Malcolm and Donalbain, and Lennox, a nobleman. They speak with a badly wounded sergeant, who has just been brought from the battlefield. He tells how Macbeth, the Thane (or Lord) of Glamis, fought and killed Macdonwald with no concern for his own safety. He also tells that the King of Norway, thinking that Scotland is losing, has joined the battle against Scotland. The sergeant is carried off for medical attention, and the Thane of Ross enters and continues the account of the battle. Macbeth's forces have won the battle. Sweno, the Norwegian king, has surrended. The Thane of Cawdor, one of Duncan's most trusted nobles, who had joined the Norwegian king, is being held for treason. Duncan sentences him to death and announces that his title, Thane of Cawdor, will be given to Macbeth.

———————◆———————

Before You Read Act I, Scene 3

The three witches meet, as they had planned earlier, and talk about what has happened since their last meeting. The First Witch met a woman, a sailor's wife, munching on chestnuts. When the witch asked for some chestnuts, the woman refused to give her any. Notice the revenge that the witch seeks against the sailor.

A drum roll announces the arrival of Macbeth. It is the end of the day, or sunset, as the witches predicted. Macbeth and Banquo, the nobleman who was co-commander in the battle, enter, and Macbeth remarks that the day has been "foul and fair." Ask yourself what he means by this. Then Banquo sees the witches.The conversation that Macbeth and Banquo have with the witches is most important. It is in this scene that the witches hint at the fate of both the noblemen. You will see that when Ross enters with Angus, another nobleman, he confirms what the witches have predicted. Macbeth and Banquo have been given a great deal to think about. Pay special attention to Banquo's warning to Macbeth ("But 'tis strange: And often-times ..."). These five lines give us the main theme of the play.

There is a connection in this scene between the First Witch's story and the witches' appearance to Macbeth. Why did Shakespeare put these two seemingly unrelated events in the same scene?

———————◆———————

ACT I. Scene 3.

Location: A heath near Forres.

[*Thunder. Enter the three* WITCHES]

FIRST WITCH.
Where hast thou been, sister?

SECOND WITCH.
Killing swine.

THIRD WITCH.
Sister, where thou?

FIRST WITCH.
A sailor's wife had chestnuts in her lap,
And munched, and munched, and munched. "Give
me," quoth I.
"Aroint thee, witch!" the rump-fed runnion cries. [1]
Her husband's to Aleppo gone, master o' the *Tiger*; [2]
But in a sieve I'll thither sail,
And like a rat without a tail [3]
I'll do, I'll do, and I'll do.

SECOND WITCH.
I'll give thee a wind.

---

1. **Aroint thee.** get away. **rump-fed.** fed on garbage, or
fat-rumped. **runnion.** mangy creature, scabby woman
2. **Aleppo.** A city in Syria, a trading center. **Tiger.** (A
ship's name.)
3. **like.** in the shape of. **without a tail.** (People believed that
witches could take the form of any animal, but the tail
would always be missing.)

FIRST WITCH.
Thou'rt kind.

THIRD WITCH.
And I another.

FIRST WITCH.
I myself have all the other,
And the very ports they blow, [4]
All the quarters that they know
I' the shipman's card. I'll drain him dry as hay. [5]
Sleep shall neither night nor day
Hang upon his penthouse lid. [6]
He shall live a man forbid. [7]
Weary sev'nnights nine times nine [8]
Shall he dwindle, peak, and pine. [9]
Though his bark cannot be lost,
Yet it shall be tempest-tossed.
Look what I have.

SECOND WITCH.
Show me, show me.

FIRST WITCH.
Herg I have a pilot's thumb,
Wrecked as homeward he did come.

[Drum within]

---

4. **they blow.** i.e., from which the winds blow. (The witches
   can prevent a ship from entering port this way.)
5. **shipman's card.** compass
6. **penthouse lid.** eyelid
7. **forbid.** accursed
8. **sev'nnights.** weeks
9. **peak.** grow thin. **pine.** waste away

THIRD WITCH.
  A drum, a drum!
  Macbeth doth come.

ALL.

  [Dancing in a circle]

  The weird Sisters, hand in hand, [10]
  Posters of the sea and land, [11]
  Thus do go about, about,
  Thrice to thine, and thrice to mine,
  And thrice again, to make up nine.
  Peace! The charm's wound up.

[Enter MACBETH and BANQUO]

MACBETH.
  So foul and fair a day I have not seen.

BANQUO.
  How far is 't called to Forres? —What are these, [12]
  So withered and so wild in their attire,
  That look not like th' inhabitants o' th' earth
  And yet are on 't? —Live you? Or are you aught [13]
  That man may question? You seem to understand me
  By each at once her chappy finger laying [14]
  Upon her skinny lips. You should be women,
  And yet your beards forbid me to interpret
  That you are so.

---

10. **weird.** connected with fate
11. **Posters of.** fast travelers over
12. **is't called.** is it said to be
13. **aught.** anything
14. **chappy.** chapped

MACBETH.

Speak, if you can. What are you?

FIRST WITCH.

All hail, Macbeth! Hail to thee, Thane of Glamis!

SECOND WITCH.

All hail, Macbeth! Hail to thee, thane of Cawdor!

THIRD WITCH.

All hail, Macbeth, that shalt be king hereafter!

BANQUO.

Good sir, why do you start and seem to fear
Things that do sound so fair? —I' the name of truth,
Are ye fantastical or that indeed [15]
Which outwardly ye show? My noble partner [16]
You greet with present grace and great prediction [17]
Of noble having and of royal hope,
That he seems rapt withal. To me you speak not. [18]
If you can look into the seeds of time
And say which grain will grow and which will not,
Speak then to me, who neither beg nor fear
Your favors nor your hate.[19]

FIRST WITCH.

Hail!

SECOND WITCH.

Hail!

THIRD WITCH.

Hail!

---

15. **fantastical.** imaginary
16. **show.** appear
17. **grace.** honor
18. **rapt.** carried away (by thought). **withal.** with it, by it
19. **beg ... hate.** beg your favors nor fear your hate

FIRST WITCH.

Lesser than Macbeth, and greater.

SECOND WITCH.

Not so happy, yet much happier. [20]

THIRD WITCH.

Thou shalt get kings, though thou be none. [21]
So all hail, Macbeth and Banquo!

FIRST WITCH.

Banquo and Macbeth, all hail!

MACBETH.

Stay, you imperfect speakers, tell me more! [22]
By Sinel's death I know I am Thane of Glamis, [23]
But how of Cawdor? The Thane of Cawdor lives
A prosperous gentleman; and to be king
Stands not within the prospect of belief,
No more than to be Cawdor. Say from whence
You owe this strange intelligence, or why [24]
Upon this blasted heath you stop our way [25]
With such prophetic greeting? Speak, I charge you.

[WITCHES *vanish*]

BANQUO.

The earth hath bubbles, as the water has,
And these are of them. Whither are they vanished?

---

20. **happy.** lucky
21. **get.** be the father of
22. **imperfect.** incomplete
23. **Sinel's.** Sinel was Macbeth's father.
24. **owe.** own, possess. **strange.** unnatural.
    intelligence. news
25. **blasted.** blighted

MACBETH.

Into the air; and what seemed corporal melted, [26]
As breath into the wind. Would they had stayed!

BANQUO.

Were such things here as we do speak about?
Or have we eaten on the insane root [27]
That takes the reason prisoner?

MACBETH.

Your children shall be kings.

BANQUO.

You shall be king.

MACBETH.

And Thane of Cawdor too. Went it not so?

BANQUO.

To th' selfsame tune and words. —Who's here?

[*Enter* ROSS *and* ANGUS]

ROSS.

The King hath happily received, Macbeth,
The news of thy success; and when he reads [28]
Thy personal venture in the rebels' sight, [29]
His wonders and his praises do contend [30]

---

26. **corporal.** real
27. **on.** of.   **insane root.** root believed to cause insanity
    (possibly mandrake, henbane, or hemlock)
28. **reads.** considers
29. **thy ... sight.** your endangering yourself before the very
    eyes of the rebels
30. **His ... that.** your wondrous deeds so outdo any praise he
    could offer that he is silenced

Which should be thine or his. Silenced with that,
In viewing o'er the rest o' the selfsame day
He finds thee in the stout Norweyan ranks,
Nothing afeard of what thyself didst make, [31]
Strange images of death. As thick as tale [32]
Came post with post, and every one did bear
Thy praises in his kingdom's great defense,
And poured them down before him.

ANGUS.
                            We are sent
To give thee from our royal master thanks,
Only to herald thee into his sight,
Not pay thee.

ROSS.
And, for an earnest of a greater honor, [33]
He bade me, from him, call thee Thane of Cawdor;
In which addition, hail, most worthy thane, [34]
For it is thine.

BANQUO.
                            What, can the devil speak true?

MACBETH.
The Thane of Cawdor lives. Why do you dress me
In borrowed robes?

---

31. Nothing ... death. Killing but not being afraid of being killed.
32. As ... with post. as fast as could be counted came messenger after messenger
33. earnest. token payment
34. addition. new title

ANGUS.
> Who was the thane lives yet, [35]
> But under heavy judgment bears that life
> Which he deserves to lose. Whether he was
>   combined [36]
> With those of Norway, or did line the rebel [37]
> With hidden help and vantage, or that with both
> He labored in his country's wrack, I know not; [38]
> But treasons capital, confessed and proved, [39]
> Have overthrown him.

MACBETH.
> [*Aside*]   Glamis, and Thane of Cawdor!
> The greatest is behind. [*To* ROSS *and* ANGUS]
> Thanks for your pains. [40]
> [*Aside to* BANQUO] Do you not hope your
>   children shall be kings
> When those that gave the Thane of Cawdor to me
> Promised no less to them?

BANQUO.
> [*To* MACBETH]   That, trusted home, [41]
> Might yet enkindle you unto the crown, [42]
> Besides the Thane of Cawdor. But 'tis strange;
> And oftentimes to win us to our harm
> The instruments of darkness tell us truths, [43]

---

35. Who. he who
36. combined. allied
37. line. support.   **the rebel.** Macdonwald
38. in. to bring about.   **wrack.** ruin
39. capital. deserving death
40. behind. still to come
41. home. all the way
42. enkindle you unto. encourage you to hope for
43. instruments of darkness. devil's workers

Win us with honest trifles, to betray's [44]
In deepest consequence.— [45]
Cousins, a word, I pray you. [46]

[*He converses apart with* ROSS *and* ANGUS]

MACBETH.
[*Aside*]   Two truths are told,
As happy prologues to the swelling act
Of the imperial theme.—I thank you, gentlemen. [47]
[*Aside*] This supernatural soliciting [48]
Cannot be ill, cannot be good. If ill,
Why hath it given me earnest of success
Commencing in a truth? I am thane of Cawdor.
If good, why do I yield to that suggestion
Whose horrid image doth unfix my hair [49]
And make my seated heart knock at my ribs,
Against the use of nature? Present fears [50]
Are less than horrible imaginings.
My thought, whose murder yet is but fantastical, [51]
Shakes so my single state of man that function [52]
Is smothered in surmise, and nothing is [53]
But what is not.

---

44. trifles. half-truths
45. In deepest consequence. in the important final
   outcome
46. Cousins. fellow lords (a term of courtesy)
47. swelling ... theme. stately idea that I will be king.
48. soliciting. tempting
49. unfix my hair. make my hair stand on end
50. use. custom. **fears.** things feared
51. whose. in which. **but fantastical.** merely imagined
52. single ... man. weak human condition. **function.**
   normal power of action
53. surmise. speculation, imaginings. **nothing ... not.** only
   unreal imaginings have (for me) any reality

BANQUO.
Look how our partner's rapt.

MACBETH.
[*Aside*]
If chance will have me king, why, chance may crown
   me
Without my stir. [54]

BANQUO.
                    New honors come upon him, [55]
Like our strange garments, cleave not to their
   mold [56]
But with the aid of use.

MACBETH.
[*Aside*]   Come what come may,
Time and the hour runs through the roughest day. [57]

BANQUO.
Worthy Macbeth, we stay upon your leisure. [58]

MACBETH.
Give me your favor. My dull brain was wrought [59]
With things forgotten. Kind gentlemen, your pains
Are registered where every day I turn [60]

---

54. **stir.** doing anything new myself.
55. **come.** which have come
56. **strange.** new.   **their mold.** the shape of the person
    within them
57. **Time ... day.** what must happen will happen one way or
    another
58. **stay.** wait
59. **favor.** pardon
60. **registered.** recorded (in my memory)

The leaf to read them. Let us toward the King.
[*Aside to* BANQUO]   Think upon what hath
    chanced, and at more time, [61]
The interim having weighed it, let us speak [62]
Our free hearts each to other. [63]

BANQUO.
    [*To* MACBETH] Very gladly.

MACBETH.
    [*To* BANQUO] Till then, enough. —Come,
    friends.

                                                        [*Exit*]

---

61. at more time. at a time of greater leisure
62. the interim ... it. when we have had time to think
    about it
63. Our free hearts. our minds freely

———————◆———————

Synopsis of Act I, Scene 3

The witches tell the story of the sailor whose voyage they will make miserable but whose ship they cannot destroy. The loss of the ship can only be brought about by the sailor's giving up hope and losing the ship. The witches then appear to Macbeth and Banquo and announce to Macbeth that he will become Thane of Cawdor and future king of Scotland. Banquo, they say, will not be king but his sons will. The witches disappear before Macbeth can question them further. Ross and Angus then confirm that Macbeth has been named Thane of Cawdor for his valor in battle. As the two men consider their futures, Banquo warns Macbeth that the powers of evil lead us on by telling the truth, but not all of it, and betray us in the final result. The witches have predicted great things for Macbeth, but how will he deal with them? He has already had thoughts of murder ("My thought, whose murder yet is but fantastical . . ."), but hopes that the witches' predictions will come true without any action on his part.

———————◆———————

---◆---

Before You Read Act I, Scene 4

In Macbeth's castle at Forres, King Duncan holds court with Lennox, Malcolm, Donalbain and his attendants. He asks if the former Thane of Cawdor has been executed. Malcolm describes his last moments and says that he was sorry for his betrayal and died bravely. Note that King Duncan still praises the traitor's character. What might this indicate about his judgment of Macbeth? Macbeth, Banquo, Ross, and Angus enter, and the King addresses Macbeth in glowing terms, saying that there is no adequate way to thank him. Macbeth confirms his loyalty to the King. The King then delivers some important news. How does Macbeth react to it? What is Macbeth thinking of when he talks to himself ("The Prince of Cumberland! That is a step ...") before exiting.

---◆---

ACT I. Scene 4.

Location: A camp near Forres.

[*Flourish. Enter* KING DUNCAN, LENNOX, MALCOLM, DONALBAIN, *and* ATTENDANTS.]

DUNCAN.
Is execution done on Cawdor? Are not
Those in commission yet returned? [1]

MALCOLM.   My liege,
They are not yet come back. But I have spoke
With one that saw him die, who did report
That very frankly he confessed his treasons,
Implored Your Highness' pardon, and set forth
A deep repentance. Nothing in his life
Became him like the leaving it. He died
As one that had been studied [2] in his death
To throw away the dearest thing he owed [3]
As 'twere a careless trifle. [4]

DUNCAN.   There's no art
To find the mind's construction in the face. [5]
He was a gentleman on whom I built
An absolute trust.

[Enter MACBETH, BANQUO, ROSS, and
ANGUS]

---

1. **in commission.** given the command (to execute Cawdor)
2. **been studied.** rehearsed
3. **owed.** owned
4. **careless.** worthless
5. **mind's construction.** person's character

O worthiest cousin!
The sin of my ingratitude even now
Was heavy on me. Thou art so far before [6]
That swiftest wing of recompense is slow
To overtake thee. Would thou hadst less deserved,
That the proportion both of thanks and payment [7]
Might have been mine! Only I have left to say,
More is thy due than more than all can pay.

MACBETH.
The service and the loyalty I owe,
In doing it, pays itself. Your Highness' part
Is to receive our duties; and our duties
Are to your throne and state children and
    servants, [8]
Which do but what they should by doing
    everything
Safe toward your love and honor. [9]
DUNCAN.
                    Welcome hither!
I have begun to plant thee, and will labor
To make thee full of growing. Noble Banquo,
That hast no less deserved, nor must be known
No less to have done so, let me infold thee
And hold thee to my heart.

BANQUO.
                    There if I grow,
The harvest is your own.

---

6. **before.** ahead (in deserving)
7. **That ... mine.** that I might have thanked and rewarded
    you according to your worth
8. **Are ... servants.** are like children and servants in relation
    to your position as king, existing only to serve you
9. **Safe toward.** with sure regard for

DUNCAN.

My plenteous joys,
Wanton in fullness, seek to hide themselves [10]
In drops of sorrow.—Sons, kinsmen, thanes,
And you whose places are the nearest, know
We will establish our estate upon [11]
Our eldest, Malcolm, whom we name hereafter
The Prince of Cumberland; which honor must [12]
Not unaccompanied invest him only, [13]
But signs of nobleness, like stars, shall shine
On all deservers.—From hence to Inverness, [14]
And bind us further to you. [15]

MACBETH.
The rest is labor which is not used for you. [16]
I'll be myself the harbinger and make joyful [17]
The hearing of my wife with your approach;
So humbly take my leave.

DUNCAN.

My worthy Cawdor!

---

10. **Wanton.** unrestrained
11. **We** (The royal "we.") **establish ... Malcolm.** make
    Malcolm the heir to my throne
12. **Prince of Cumberland.** (title of the heir apparent to
    the Scottish throne)
13. **Not ... only.** not be given to Malcolm alone; other
    deserving nobles are to share honors
14. **Inverness.** Macbeth's castle
15. **bind ... you.** put me further in your (Macbeth's) debt by
    your hospitality
16. **The ... you.** even rest, when not devoted to your service,
    becomes work
17. **harbinger.** advance messenger to arrange royal lodging

MACBETH. [*Aside*]
   The Prince of Cumberland! That is a step
   On which I must fall down or else o'erleap,
   For in my way it lies. Stars, hide your fires; [18]
   Let not light see my black and deep desires.
   The eye wink at the hand? yet let that be [19]
   Which the eye fears, when it is done, to see.

   [*Exit*]

DUNCAN.
   True, worthy Banquo. He is full so valiant, [20]
   And in his commendations I am fed;
   It is a banquet to me. Let's after him,
   Whose care is gone before to bid us welcome.
   It is a peerless kinsman.

   [*Flourish*] [*Exit*]

---

18. **in my way it lies.** (the monarchy was not hereditary,
    and Macbeth had a right to believe that he himself might
    be chosen as Duncan's successor; he here questions
    whether he will interfere with the course of events.)
19. **wink ... hand.** don't let the eye see what the hand is
    doing; let that be done which the eye fears to look at after
    it has been done
20. **full so valiant.** as brave as you say

---◆---

Synopsis of Act I, Scene 4

Both King Duncan and Macbeth expressed their loyalty to one another in the previous scene. Duncan's announcement that he has named his oldest son as the next king, causes Macbeth to wonder about the witches' prediction that he will be king. As he leaves the king to notify his wife, Lady Macbeth, that the king is coming to their castle, Macbeth again hints at dark deeds to come. ("Stars, hide your fires; Let not light see my black and deep desires ...") Duncan comments to Banquo on Macbeth's fine character and says he looks forward to the banquet at Macbeth's castle.

---◆---

Before You Read Act I, Scene 5

In Macbeth's castle at Inverness, Lady
Macbeth reads a letter from Macbeth which tells of
the witches' predictions and of his immediate
appointment as Thane of Cawdor. She reacts quickly to the news and decides what Macbeth must do.
What are her doubts about Macbeth? A messenger
arrives from Macbeth and tells her that the King
will be there that night. When Macbeth himself
arrives only moments later, Lady Macbeth has
already decided what they must do.

ACT I. Scene 5.

Location: Inverness. Macbeth's castle.

[*Enter* MACBETH'S WIFE, *alone, with a letter*]

LADY MACBETH. [*Reads*]

"They met me in the day of success; and I have
learned by the perfect'st [1] report they have more in
them than mortal know-ledge. When I burnt in
desire to question them further, they made themselves air, into which they vanished. Whiles I stood
rapt in the wonder of it came missives [2] from the
King, who all-hailed me 'thane of Cawdor,' by which
title, before, these weird sisters saluted me, and
referred me to the coming on of time with 'Hail,
king, that shalt be!' This have I thought good to
deliver [3] thee, my dearest partner of greatness, that
thou mightst not lose the dues of rejoicing by being
ignorant of what greatness is promised thee. Lay it
to thy heart, and farewell."

Glamis thou art, and Cawdor, and shalt be
What thou art promised. Yet do I fear thy nature? [4]
It is too full o' the milk of human kindness
To catch the nearest way. Thou wouldst be great,
Art not without ambition, but without
The illness should attend it. What thou wouldst
    highly, [5]

---

1. **perfect'st.** most accurate
2. **missives.** messengers
3. **deliver.** inform
4. **fear.** am worried about, mistrust
5. **illness.** evil (which) ... **highly.** greatly

That wouldst thou holily; wouldst not play false,
And yet wouldst wrongly win. Thou'dst have,
  great Glamis,
That which cries "Thus thou must do," if thou
  have it, [6]
And that which rather thou dost fear to do [7]
Than wishest should be undone. Hie thee hither, [8]
That I may pour my spirits in thine ear
And chastise with the valor of my tongue
All that impedes thee from the golden round [9]
Which fate and metaphysical aid doth seem [10]
To have thee crowned withal. [11]

[*Enter* MESSENGER]
                              What is your tidings?
MESSENGER.
The King comes here tonight.

LADY MACBETH.
                              Thou'rt mad to say it!
Is not thy master with him, who, were't so,
Would have informed for preparation? [12]

---

6. have. are to have, want to have
7. And that ... undone and the thing you most want
   frightens you more in terms of the means needed to get it
   than in the idea of having it; if you could have it without
   those means, you certainly wouldn't wish it undone
8. Hie. hasten
9. round. crown
10. metaphysical. supernatural
11. withal. with
12. informed for preparation. let me know so that I
   might get things ready

MESSENGER.
So please you, it is true. Our thane is coming.
One of my fellows had the speed of him, [13]
Who, almost dead for breath, had scarcely more
Than would make up his message.

LADY MACBETH.
                                    Give him tending; [14]
He brings great news.

                              [*Exit* MESSENGER]
                    The raven himself is hoarse
That croaks the fatal entrance of Duncan
Under my battlements. Come, you spirits
That tend on mortal thoughts, unsex me here [15]
And fill me from the crown to the toe top-full
Of direst cruelty! Make thick my blood;
Stop up th' access and passage to remorse,
That no compunctious visitings of nature [17]
Shake my fell purpose, nor keep peace between [18]
Th' effect and it! Come to my woman's breasts [19]
And take my milk for gall, you murdering
     ministers, [20]
Wherever in your sightless substances [21]

---

13. **had ... of.** overtook
14. **tending.** attendance
15. **tend ... thoughts.** attend on, bring about deadly or
     murderous thoughts
16. **remorse.** pity
17. **nature.** natural feelings
18. **fell.** cruel.   **keep peace.** interfere with
19. **Th' effect and it.** my evil purpose and doing it
20. **for gall.** in exchange for bitterness.   **ministers.** agents
21. **sightless.** invisible

You wait on nature's mischief! Come, thick night, [22]
And pall thee in the dunnest smoke of hell, [23]
That my keen knife see not the wound it makes,
Nor heaven peep through the blanket of the dark
To cry "Hold, hold!"

[*Enter* MACBETH]
                Great Glamis! Worthy Cawdor!
Greater than both by the all-hail hereafter!
Thy letters have transported me beyond [24]
This ignorant present, and I feel now
The future in the instant.

MACBETH.
                My dearest love,
Duncan comes here tonight.

LADY MACBETH.
                   And when goes hence?

MACBETH.
Tomorrow, as he purposes.

LADY MACBETH.
                  O, never
Shall sun that morrow see!
Your face, my thane, is as a book where men
May read strange matters. To beguile the time,
Look like the time; bear welcome in your eye, [26]

---

22. **wait on'.** attend, assist. **nature's mischief.** evil done to
    nature, or within the realm of nature
23. **pall.** envelop.   **dunnest.** darkest
24. **letters have.** letter has
25. **beguile the time.** deceive the people tonight
26. **Look like the time.** look the way people expect you to look

Your hand, your tongue. Look like th' innocent
  flower,
But be the serpent under 't. He that's coming
Must be provided for; and you shall put
This night's great business into my dispatch, [27]
Which shall to all our nights and days to come
Give solely sovereign sway and masterdom.

MACBETH.
We will speak further.

LADY MACBETH.
                          Only look up clear. [28]
To alter favor ever is to fear. [29]
Leave all the rest to me.

                                    [*Exit*]

---

27. **dispatch.** management
28. **look up clear.** give the appearance of being innocent
29. **To ... fear.** to show a troubled face will arouse suspicion

---◆---

Synopsis of Act I, Scene 5

It is clear from the last scene that Lady Macbeth is ruthless. She will commit any crime to get what she wants. Her only fear is that Macbeth might shrink from murder. When Macbeth arrives at the castle, she is calling on supernatural spirits ("Come you spirits That tend on mortal thoughts ...") to free her from any thoughts of mercy or morality. When Macbeth tells her that Duncan plans to leave the next day, she says that Duncan will never see the next day. Macbeth exits without commenting on her plans. She tells him to look innocent and leave everything to her.

---◆---

---◆---

Before You Read Act I, Scene 6

This scene outside Macbeth's castle contrasts with what is going on in the castle (and what *will* happen in the castle). Shakespeare is showing us how different King Duncan and Banquo are from their hosts, Macbeth and Lady Macbeth. Does Lady Macbeth give the King any reason to think twice before accepting her hospitality?

---◆---

ACT I. Scene 6.

Location: Before Macbeth's castle.

[*Hautboys and torches.* *Enter* KING DUNCAN, MALCOLM, DONALBAIN, BANQUO, LENNOX, MACDUFF, ROSS, ANGUS, *and* ATTENDANTS] [1]

DUNCAN.
This castle hath a pleasant seat. The air [2]
Nimbly and sweetly recommends itself
Unto our gentle senses. [3]

BANQUO.
This guest of summer,
The temple-haunting martlet, does approve [4]
By his loved mansionry that the heaven's breath [5]
Smells wooingly here. No jutty, frieze, [6]
Buttress, nor coign of vantage but this bird [7]
Hath made his pendent bed and procreant cradle. [8]
Where they most breed and haunt, I have observed
The air is delicate.

[*Enter* LADY MACBETH]

---

1. **Hautboys.** musical instruments like oboes
2. **seat.** location
3. **gentle.** soothed
4. **temple-haunting.** nesting in churches.
   martlet. house martin. **approve.** prove
5. **mansionry.** nests
6. **jutty.** projection of wall or building
7. **coign of vantage.** convenient corner, i.e., for nesting
8. **procreant.** for breeding

DUNCAN.

See, see, our honored hostess!
The love that follows us sometimes is our trouble, [9]
Which still we thank as love. Herein I teach you
How you shall bid God 'ild us for your pains, [10]
And thank us for your trouble.

LADY MACBETH.

All our service
In every point twice done, and then done double,
Were poor and single business to contend [11]
Against those honors deep and broad wherewith
Your Majesty loads our house. For those of old, [12]
And the late dignities heaped up to them, [13]
We rest your hermits. [14]

DUNCAN.

Where's the Thane of Cawdor?
We coursed him at the heels, and had a purpose [15]
To be his purveyor; but he rides well, [16]
And his great love, sharp as his spur, hath holp him [17]

---

9. **The love ... love.** we appreciate even love we may not
   want, since it is meant as love. (Duncan is saying that
   his visit is a bother, but, he hopes, a welcome one.)
10. **bid ... pains.** ask God to pay me back for the trouble I'm
    giving you.
11. **single.** small. **contend Against.** compete with
12. **those of old.** honors formerly given to us
13. **late.** recent. **to.** besides, in addition to
14. **rest.** remain. **hermits.** those who will pray for you
    like hermits. (Hermits were often paid to pray for
    another person's soul.)
15. **coursed.** followed (as in a hunt)
16. **purveyor.** advance supply officer
17. **holp.** helped

To his home before us. Fair and noble hostess,
We are your guest tonight.

LADY MACBETH.
                                    Your servants ever
Have theirs, themselves, and what is theirs in
        compt [18]
To make their audit at your Highness' pleasure, [19]
Still to return your own. [20]

DUNCAN.
                                Give me your hand.
Conduct me to mine host. We love him highly, [21]
And shall continue our graces towards him.
By your leave, hostess.

                                                    [Exit]

---

18. **Have theirs.** have their servants.   **what is theirs.** their wealth, possessions.   **in compt.** in trust
19. **make their audit.** submit their account (for the King's approval)
20. **Still.** always.   **return your own.** merely give back what is yours, since we hold it in trust from you.
21. **We.** (The royal "we.")

Synopsis of Act I, Scene 6

King Duncan arrives in front of Macbeth's castle in the evening with Malcolm, Donalbain, Banquo, Lennox, Macduff, Ross, Angus and their servants. The King comments on the beautiful countryside and the pleasant breezes. Banquo agrees with him in a charming speech about the summer season. Lady Macbeth comes out of the castle, and the King thanks her for her trouble. She says that she will do the best she can to honor the King. Duncan asks where Macbeth is, and Lady Macbeth conducts him into the castle

Before You Read Act I, Scene 7

Macbeth has strong doubts about his wife's plan to kill King Duncan. What are some of the problems he is worried about? When he expresses his doubts to Lady Macbeth, She wants to know why he has given up his plans to be king. When Macbeth says he cannot go through with the murder, Lady Macbeth tells him something about her character that is an important element in the tragedy. Who will kill Duncan? Who will be blamed for the murder?

ACT I. Scene 7.

Location: Macbeth's castle; an inner courtyard.

[*Hautboys. Torches. Enter a* SEWER,[1] *and divers* SERVANTS *with dishes and service, and pass over the stage. Then enter* MACBETH]

MACBETH.
If it were done when 'tis done, then 'twere well [2]
It were done quickly. If th' assassination
Could trammel up the consequence and catch [3]
With his surcease success-that but this blow [4]
Might be the be-all and the end-all!—here, [5]
But here, upon this bank and shoal of time,
We'd jump the life to come. But in these cases [6]
We still have judgment here, that we but teach [7]
Bloody instructions, which, being taught, return [8]
To plague th' inventor. This evenhanded justice
Commends th' ingredients of our poisoned chalice [9]
To our own lips. He's here in double trust:

---

1. **sewer.** chief butler
2. **done ... done.** over and done with after it's done
3. **trammel ... consequence.** entangle in a net and prevent the resulting events
4. **his surcease.** cessation (of the assassination and of Duncan's life). **success.** what succeeds, follows
5. **here.** in this world
6. **jump.** risk
7. **still have judgment.** are always punished. **that.** in that
8. **instructions.** lessons
9. **Commends.** offers. **ingredients.** contents of a mixture. **chalice.** cup

First, as I am his kinsman and his subject,
Strong both against the deed; then, as his host,
Who should against his murderer shut the door,
Not bear the knife myself. Besides, this Duncan
Hath borne his faculties so meek, hath been [10]
So clear in his great office, that his virtues [11]
Will plead like angels, trumpet-tongued, against
The deep damnation of his taking-off; [12]
And Pity, like a naked newborn babe
Striding the blast, or heaven's cherubin, horsed [13]
Upon the sightless couriers of the air, [14]
Shall blow the horrid deed in every eye,
That tears shall drown the wind. I have no spur [15]
To prick the sides of my intent, but only
Vaulting ambition, which o'erleaps itself
And falls on th' other— [16]

[*Enter* LADY MACBETH]

How now, what news?

LADY MACBETH.
He has almost supped. Why have you left the
chamber?

---

10. **faculties.** powers of office
11. **clear.** without blame
12. **taking-off.** murder
13. **Striding.** bestriding
14. **sightless couriers.** invisible horses or runners, i.e., the winds
15. **shall drown the wind.** will be as heavy as a downpour of rain, which stills the wind
16. **other.** other side.   (The idea is of a man jumping into his saddle and falling off the opposite side.)

MACBETH.
Hath he asked for me?

LADY MACBETH.
Know you not he has?

MACBETH.
We will proceed no further in this business.
He hath honored me of late, and I have bought [17]
Golden opinions from all sorts of people,
Which would be worn now in their newest gloss, [18]
Not cast aside so soon.

LADY MACBETH.
Was the hope drunk
Wherein you dressed yourself? Hath it slept since?
And wakes it now, to look so green and pale [19]
At what it did so freely? From this time
Such I account thy love. Art thou afeard
To be the same in thine own act and valor
As thou art in desire? Wouldst thou have that
Which thou esteem'st the ornament of life, [20]
And live a coward in thine own esteem,
Letting "I dare not" wait upon "I would," [21]
Like the poor cat i' th' adage? [22]

---

17. bought. acquired (by bravery in battle)
18. would. ought to
19. green. sickly
20. the ornament of life. the crown
21. wait upon. follow
22. adage. from an old saying about a cat who wants to eat
fish but is afraid of getting its paws wet.

MACBETH.

Prithee, peace!
I dare do all that may become a man;
Who dares do more is none.

LADY MACBETH.

What beast was 't, then,
That made you break this enterprise to me? [23]
When you durst do it, then you were a man;
And to be more than what you were, you would
Be so much more the man. Nor time nor place
Did then adhere, and yet you would make both. [24]
They have made themselves, and that their fitness
    now [25]
Does unmake you. I have given suck, and know
How tender 'tis to love the babe that milks me;
I would, while it was smiling in my face,
Have plucked my nipple from his boneless gums
And dashed the brains out, had I so sworn as you
Have done to this.

MACBETH.

If we should fail?

LADY MACBETH.

We fail?
But screw your courage to the sticking place [26]
And we'll not fail. When Duncan is asleep—

---

23. **break.** broach
24. **Did ... adhere.** was then suitable for the assassination.
    would. wanted to
25. **that their fitness.** their very suitability
26. **But.** only. **the sticking place.** the notch that holds
    the bowstring of a crossbow tightly stretched for shooting

Whereto the rather shall his day's hard journey
Soundly invite him—his two chamberlains [27]
Will I with wine and wassail so convince [28]
That memory, the warder of the brain, [29]
Shall be a fume, and the receipt of reason [30]
A limbeck only. When in swinish sleep [31]
Their drenchèd natures lies as in a death,
What cannot you and I perform upon
Th' unguarded Duncan? What not put upon
His spongy officers, who shall bear the guilt [32]
Of our great quell? [33]

MACBETH.

                Bring forth men-children only!
For thy undaunted mettle should compose [34]
Nothing but males. Will it not be received, [35]
When we have marked with blood those sleepy two
Of his own chamber and used their very daggers,
That they have done 't?

---

27. chamberlains. servants in the bedroom
28. wassail. drink. **convince.** overpower
29. warder ... only. (The brain was thought to be divided
    into three parts, imagination in front, memory at the
    back, and between them the seat of reason. The fumes of
    wine, arising from the stomach, would deaden memory
    and judgment.)
30. receipt. thing that receives
31. limbeck. still
32. spongy. soaked, drunken
33. quell. murder
34. mettle. character
35. received. as truth

LADY MACBETH.

Who dares receive it other, [36]
As we shall make our griefs and clamor roar [37]
Upon his death?

MACBETH.

I am settled, and bend up [38]
Each corporal agent to this terrible feat.
Away, and mock the time with fairest show. [39]
False face must hide what the false heart doth
know.

[Exit]

---

36. other. otherwise
37. As. inasmuch as
38. bend ... agent. strain every muscle
39. mock. deceive

Synopsis of Act I, Scene 7

In Macbeth's castle, servants prepare for the banquet for Duncan. Macbeth enters and gives us his thoughts on the murder of Duncan. He wishes the murder could be committed without any resulting problems. He knows how hard it is to get away with crimes. He also realizes that Duncan is not only his king but his relative. At the moment, Duncan is his guest, and it is Macbeth's duty to protect him. Duncan has been a good king and has shown great generosity to Macbeth. Finally, Macbeth fears the judgment that Heaven will pass on him. However, he feels that his ambition may enable him to go through with the murder. Lady Macbeth comes in and asks Macbeth why he is not with the King. When Macbeth expresses his doubts about killing Duncan, Lady Macbeth accuses him of not being honest with himself about what he wants. How does she know this? She says that although she is a woman, she has the nerve to act when she knows what she wants. ("What beast was 't then That made you break this enterprise to me?") Notice, though, how she pursuades Macbeth that he should commit the murder. ("But screw your courage to the sticking-place And we'll not fail.") She assures him that she will help him with the murder. Lady Macbeth will put a sleeping potion in the bedtime drinks of two of Duncan's servants. When they fall asleep, Macbeth will use their daggers to kill Duncan in his sleep. He will then put their daggers back on them and smear them with Duncan's blood. Macbeth is shocked by her plan but he also thinks it will work. He agrees to murder Duncan.

———————◆———————

MACBETH.
That will never be.
Who can impress the forest, bid the tree [34]
Unfix his earthbound root? Sweet bodements,
    good! [35]
Rebellious dead, rise never till the wood [36]
Of Birnam rise, and our high-placed Macbeth
Shall live the lease of nature, pay his breath [37]
To time and mortal custom. Yet my heart [38]
Throbs to know one thing. Tell me, if your art
Can tell so much: shall Banquo's issue ever
Reign in this kingdom?

ALL.
Seek to know no more.

MACBETH.
I will be satisfied. Deny me this,
And an eternal curse fall on you! Let me know.

[*The cauldron descends. Hautboys*]

Why sinks that cauldron? And what noise is this? [39]

FIRST WITCH.
Show!

SECOND WITCH.
Show!

---

34. **impress.** press into service, like soldiers
35. **bodements.** prophecies
36. **Rebellious dead.** Banquo and his descendents
37. **lease of nature.** natural lifespan
38. **mortal custom.** natural death
39. **noise.** music

THIRD WITCH.
Show!

ALL.
Show his eyes, and grieve his heart;
Come like shadows, so depart!

[*A show of eight* KINGS *and* BANQUO *last, the eighth King, with a glass in his hand*] [40]

MACBETH.
Thou art too like the spirit of Banquo. Down!
Thy crown does sear mine eyeballs. And thy hair,
Thou other gold-bound brow, is like the first. [41]
A third is like the former. Filthy hags,
Why do you show me this? A fourth? Start, eyes! [42]
What, will the line stretch out to th' crack of doom?
Another yet? A seventh? I'll see no more.
And yet the eighth appears, who bears a glass
Which shows me many more; and some I see
That twofold balls and treble scepters carry. [43]
Horrible sight! Now I see 'tis true,
For the blood-boltered Banquo smiles upon me [44]
And points at them for his. [45] [*The* APPARITIONS
    vanish]
What, is this so?

---

40. **glass.** mirror
41. **other.** second
42. **Start.** bulge from their sockets
43. **twofold balls.** probably refers to the double coronation
    of James as King of England and Scotland.)
    treble scepters. probably refers to James's title as King
    of Great Britain, France, and Ireland.)
44. **blood-boltered.** with his hair matted with blood
45. **for his.** as his descendants

FIRST WITCH.
Ay, sir, all this is so. But why
Stands Macbeth thus amazedly? [46]
Come, sisters, cheer we up his sprites [47]
And show the best of our delights.
I'll charm the air to give a sound,
While you perform your antic round, [48]
That this great king may kindly say
Our duties did his welcome pay. [49]

[*Music. The* WITCHES *dance, and vanish*]

MACBETH.
Where are they? Gone? Let this pernicious hour
Stand aye accursèd in the calendar!
Come in, without there!

[*Enter* LENNOX]

LENNOX.
                        What's Your Grace's will?

MACBETH.
Saw you the Weird Sisters?

LENNOX.
                        No, my lord.

MACBETH.
Came they not by you?

---

46. amazedly. stunned
47. sprites. spirits
48. antic round. grotesque dance in a circle
49. pay. repay

LENNOX.

No, indeed, my lord.

MACBETH.
Infected be the air whereon they ride,
And damned all those that trust them! I did hear
The galloping of horse. Who was 't came by? [50]

LENNOX.
'Tis two or three, my lord, that bring you word
Macduff is fled to England.

MACBETH.

Fled to England!

LENNOX.
Ay, my good lord.

MACBETH.
[Aside]
Time, thou anticipat'st my dread exploits. [51]
The flighty purpose never is o'ertook [52]
Unless the deed go with it. From this moment
The very firstlings of my heart shall be [53]
The firstlings of my hand. And even now,
To crown my thoughts with acts, be it thought and
   done:
The castle of Macduff I will surprise, [54]

---

50. **horse.** horses
51. **thou anticipat'st.** you foretold.
52. **The flighty ... it.** The fleeting plan is never fulfilled
   unless it is carried out at once.
53. **The very ... hand.** my impulses will be acted on
   immediately
54. **surprise.** seize without warning

Seize upon Fife, give to th' edge o' the sword
His wife, his babes, and all unfortunate souls
That trace him in his line.   No boasting like
    a fool; [55]
This deed I'll do before this purpose cool.
But no more sights! —Where are these gentlemen?
Come, bring me where they are.

                                        [*Exit*]

---

55. **trace him.** follow his tracks.   **line.** family succession

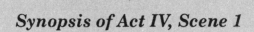

Synopsis of Act IV, Scene 1

After the witches have finished most of the recipe for their brew, Hecate congragulates them on their efforts. Macbeth enters and says that he wants them to give him more information about what will happen to him, no matter what strange disasters may result. The First Witch asks Macbeth if he will hear the information from their "masters." When he replies yes, the witches throw some additional ingredients into their brew, and the first of three apparitions, a head wearing a helmet, appears. Macbeth speaks to the head, but the witches tell him to be quiet, that the apparition knows Macbeth's thoughts. The First Apparition tells Macbeth to beware of the Thane of Fife, that is, Macduff. The Second Apparition is a bloody child. It tells Macbeth not to be afraid of other men because "none of woman born" will harm him. Macbeth is first satisfied to let Macduff live, but then he changes his mind and decides to kill him. The Third Apparition is a child wearing a crown and holding a tree in his hand. This apparition tells Macbeth that he will not be defeated until the Forest of Birnam moves to Dunsinane. Macbeth remarks on the impossibility of a forest moving and decides he will live into old age. Macbeth still is not satisfied, however, and he demands to know if Banquo's sons will really be kings of Scotland, as the witches predicted earlier. The witches summon up a vision of Banquo with eight kings. The last king holds a mirror in his hand. As the kings appear, one by one, confirming the line of kings that Banquo will establish, Macbeth becomes increasingly angry. The witches pretend to be surprised by his anger, and they sing and dance before they vanish. Lennox then enters and informs him that Macduff has left for England. Macbeth resolves to have Macduff killed, along with his wife and children, and anyone else related to Macduff who might carry on his family.

———————◆———————

Before You Read Act IV, Scene 2

This is a sad and upsetting scene. It gives us some idea of the horror that Macbeth has brought to Scotland. We find out that Lady Macduff, Macduff's wife, does not know why her husband has left for England. What does she think about Macduff's leaving? Notice the tone of the conversation between Lady Macduff and her son. Why do you think Shakespeare shows us this side of Lady Macduff and her son at this point in the scene?

ACT IV. Scene 2.

Location: Fife. Macduff's castle.

[*Enter MACDUFF'S WIFE, her SON, and ROSS*]

LADY MACDUFF.
What had he done to make him fly the land?

ROSS.
You must have patience, madam.

LADY MACDUFF.
        He had none.
His flight was madness. When our actions do not, [1]
Our fears do make us traitors.

ROSS.
        You know not
Whether it was his wisdom or his fear.

LADY MACDUFF.
Wisdom? to leave his wife, to leave his babes,
His mansion, and his titles in a place [2]
From whence himself does fly? He loves us not,
He wants the natural touch; for the poor wren, [3]
The most diminutive of birds, will fight,
Her young ones in her nest, against the owl. [4]
All is the fear and nothing is the love,

---

1. **when ... traitors.** even when we have not committed treason, our fears of being suspected as traitors make us act as if we were
2. **titles.** i.e., possessions to which he has title
3. **wants.** lacks. **the natural touch.** the feelings natural to a husband and father
4. **Her ... nest.** when her young ones are in the nest

As little is the wisdom, where the flight
So runs against all reason.

ROSS.

My dearest coz, [5]
I pray you, school yourself. But, for your husband, [6]
The fits o' the season. I dare not speak much
    further, [7]
But cruel are the times when we are traitors [8]
And do not know ourselves, when we hold rumor
From what we fear, yet know not what we fear, [9]
But float upon a wild and violent sea
Each way and none. I take my leave of you; [10]
Shall not be long but I'll be here again. [11]
Things at the worst will cease, or else climb upward
To what they were before. —My pretty cousin,
Blessing upon you!

LADY MACDUFF.
Fathered he is, and yet he's fatherless.

ROSS.
I am so much a fool, should I stay longer

---

5. **coz.** kinswoman
6. **school.** control.   **for.** as for
7. **fits 'o the season.** disorders of the time
8. **are traitors ... ourselves.** are accused of treason
    without recognizing ourselves as such
9. **hold ... fear.** believe every frightening rumor on the
    basis of our fears
10. **Each ... none.** being tossed this way and that without
    any real progress
11. **Shall.** it shall.   **but.** before
12. **It ... discomfort.** I should disgrace myself by weeping,
    and embarrass you

It would be my disgrace and your discomfort. [12]
I take my leave at once.

[*Exit ROSS*]

LADY MACDUFF.
Sirrah, your father's dead; [13]
And what will you do now? How will you live?

SON.
As birds do, Mother.

LADY MACDUFF.
What, with worms and flies?

SON.
With what I get, I mean; and so do they.

LADY MACDUFF.
Poor bird! Thou'dst never fear
The net nor lime, the pitfall nor the gin. [14]

SON.
Why should I, Mother? Poor birds they are not set
for.[15]
My father is not dead, for all your saying.

LADY MACDUFF.
Yes, he is dead. How wilt thou do for a father?

SON.
Nay, how will you do for a husband?

---

13. Sirrah. (here, an affectionate form of address to a child.)
14. lime. birdlime (a sticky substance put on branches to
snare birds). **gin.** trap
15. Poor ... for. traps are not set for *poor* birds, as you call
me

LADY MACDUFF.
Why, I can buy me twenty at any
market.

SON.
Then you'll buy 'em to sell again.

LADY MACDUFF.
Thou speak'st with all thy wit,
And yet, i' faith, with wit enough for thee.

SON.
Was my father a traitor, Mother?

LADY MACDUFF.
Ay, that he was.

SON.
What is a traitor?

LADY MACDUFF.
Why, one that swears and lies. [16]

SON.
And be all traitors that do so?

LADY MACDUFF.
Every one that does so is a traitor,
And must be hanged.

SON.
And must they all be hanged that swear and lie?

LADY MACDUFF.
Every one.

---

16. swears and lies. swears an oath and breaks it

SON.
Who must hang them?

LADY MACDUFF.
Why, the honest men.

SON.
Then the liars and swearers are fools, for there are
liars and swearers enough to beat the honest
men and hang up them.

LADY MACDUFF.
Now, God help thee, poor monkey! But how wilt
thou do for a father?

SON.
If he were dead, you'd weep for him; if you would
not, it were a good sign that I should quickly
have a new father.

LADY MACDUFF.
Poor prattler, how thou talk'st!

[Enter a MESSENGER]

MESSENGER.
Bless you, fair dame! I am not to you known,
Though in your state of honor I am perfect. [17]
I doubt some danger does approach you nearly. [18]
If you will take a homely man's advice, [19]
Be not found here. Hence with your little ones!
To fright you thus, methinks, I am too savage;

---

17. **in ... perfect.** I am fully informed of your honorable rank.
18. **doubt.** fear
19. **homely.** plain

To do worse to you were fell cruelty, [20]
Which is too nigh your person. Heaven preserve
    you! [21]
I dare abide no longer.

[Exit MESSENGER]

LADY MACDUFF.

Whither should I fly?
I have done no harm. But I remember now
I am in this earthly world, where to do harm
Is often laudable, to do good sometimes
Accounted dangerous folly. Why then, alas,
Do I put up that womanly defense
To say I have done no harm?

[Enter MURDERERS]

What are these faces?

FIRST MURDERER.
Where is your husband?

LADY MACDUFF.
I hope in no place so unsanctified
Where such as thou mayst find him.

FIRST MURDERER.

He's a traitor.

SON.
Thou liest, thou shag-haired villain!

FIRST MURDERER.

What, you egg?

---

20. **To do worse.** actually to harm you. **fell.** fierce
21. **Which ... person.** which is all too near at hand

[*He stabs him*]

Young fry of treachery! [22]

SON.

He has killed me, Mother.
Run away, I pray you!

[*He dies*]

[*Exit LADY MACDUFF crying "Murder!"*
followed by the MURDERERS with the SON'S
body]

---

22. fry. offspring

---◆---

Synopsis of Act IV, Scene 2

At Macduff's castle, Lady Macduff enters with her son and Ross. She is discussing with Ross why her husband, Macduff, has gone to England without saying goodbye or telling her why he left. She is upset and cannot understand why he should leave her and the children alone with no explanation. Ross tells her that she should have patience. He reminds her that Macduff is a smart man and has good judgment. He may have had good reasons to leave in this way, Ross suggests. Lady Macduff is too upset for this explanation. Ross himself is so moved by her distress that he tells her that he must leave before he begins to weep. In her despair and desperation, Lady Macduff turns to her son and tells him, half seriously, half humorously, that his father is dead. How will they live? she asks him. Catching the tone of her question, he replies that they will live like birds, on what they can find. Their conversation continues in this vein, with the young boy's questions revealing a combination of intelligence and innocence. Suddenly, a messenger arrives and warns her that danger is near. He tells Lady Macduff that she should leave and hide immediately. He then leaves himself. Lady Macduff says that she has done no one any harm, and that she has nowhere to go in any case. Murderers come into the room, and one of them asks her where Macduff is. She says she hopes he is in no place the murderers would know about, because that

---◆---

would be an evil place indeed. The murderer says that Macduff is a traitor. Macduff's son insults the murderer and calls him a liar. At this the murderer stabs the boy, who tells his mother to run. Lady Macduff runs out, followed by the murderers, screaming "Murder!"

---◆---

Before You Read Act IV, Scene 3

Act IV, Scene 3 consists entirely of conversation and offers some relief from the nonstop action of most of the preceding scenes. This is the longest scene in Macbeth, and it falls into three parts. First there is a discussion between Macduff and Malcolm about the conditions in Scotland. Notice how Malcolm describes the kind of king he (Malcolm) will be. How does Macduff react to this description? During the second part, a doctor comes on stage and describes some unusual powers possessed by King Edward of England. Third, Ross arrives from Scotland with terrible news for Macduff. Pay attention to the reactions of the various characters in this very emotional part of the scene.

---◆---

ACT IV. Scene 3.

Location: England. Before King Edward the Confessor's palace.

[*Enter* MALCOLM *and* MACDUFF]

MALCOLM.
Let us seek out some desolate shade, and there
Weep our sad bosoms empty.

MACDUFF.
                              Let us rather
Hold fast the mortal sword, and like good men [1]
Bestride our downfall'n birthdom. Each new morn [2]
New widows howl, new orphans cry, new sorrows
Strike heaven on the face, that it resounds [3]
As if it felt with Scotland and yelled out [4]
Like syllable of dolor.[5]

MALCOLM.
                       What I believe, I'll wail;
What know, believe; and what I can redress, [6]

---

1. **mortal.** deadly
2. **Bestride.** stand over in defense. **birthdom.** native land
3. **Strike ... face.** give an insulting slap in the face to heaven itself. **that it resounds.** so that it echoes
4. **As ... dolor.** as if heaven, feeling itself the blow delivered to Scotland, cried out with a similar cry of pain
5. **Like.** similar.
6. **What ... believe.** what I believe to be wrong in Scotland I will grieve for, and anything I am certain to be true I will believe.

As I shall find the time to friend, I will. [7]
What you have spoke it may be so, perchance.
This tyrant, whose sole name blisters our tongues, [8]
Was once thought honest. You have loved him well;
He hath not touched you yet. I am young; but something [9]
You may deserve of him through me, and wisdom [10]
To offer up a weak, poor, innocent lamb
T' appease an angry god.

MACDUFF.
I am not treacherous.

MALCOLM.
But Macbeth is.
A good and virtuous nature may recoil [11]
In an imperial charge. But I shall crave your
pardon. [12]
That which you are my thoughts cannot transpose; [13]
Angels are bright still, though the brightest fell. [14]
Though all things foul would wear the brows of
grace, [15]

---

7. **to friend.** be friendly
8. **sole.** very
9. **He ... yet.** the fact that Macbeth hasn't hurt you yet makes me suspicious of you. **young.** inexperienced. **something ... me.** you may earn favor with Macbeth by betraying me to him
10. **wisdom.** it is wise
11. **recoil.** give way
12. **In ... charge.** under pressure from royal command.
13. **That ... transpose.** my suspicious thoughts cannot change you from what you are
14. **brightest.** brightest angel, i.e., Lucifer
15. **Though ... so.** even though evil puts on the appearance of good so often as to make that appearance suspicious, yet goodness must go on looking and acting like itself

Yet grace must still look so.

MACDUFF.

I have lost my hopes. [16]

MALCOLM.

Perchance even there where I did find my doubts. [17]
Why in that rawness left you wife and child, [18]
Those precious motives, those strong knots of love, [19]
Without leave-taking? I pray you,
Let not my jealousies be your dishonors, [20]
But mine own safeties. You may be rightly just,
Whatever I shall think.

MACDUFF.

Bleed, bleed, poor country!
Great tyranny, lay thou thy basis sure, [21]
For goodness dare not check thee? wear thou thy
    wrongs, [22]
The title is affeered! Fare thee well, lord. [23]
I would not be the villain that thou think'st
For the whole space that's in the tyrant's grasp,
And the rich East to boot. [24]

---

16. **hopes.** hopes of Malcolm's help in the cause against
    Macbeth
17. **Perchance even there.** perhaps with that same
    mistrust. **doubts.** fears such as that Macduff may
    secretly be on Macbeth's side
18. **rawness.** unprotected condition
19. **motives.** reasons to offer strong protection
20. **Let ... safeties.** may it be true that my suspicions of
    your lack of honor are founded only in my own caution
21. **basis.** foundation
22. **wrongs.** wrongfully gained powers
23. **affeered.** confirmed, certified
24. **to boot.** in addition

MALCOLM.

Be not offended.
I speak not as in absolute fear of you. [25]
I think our country sinks beneath the yoke; [26]
It weeps, it bleeds, and each new day a gash
Is added to her wounds. I think withal [27]
There would be hands uplifted in my right; [28]
And here from gracious England have I offer [29]
Of goodly thousands. But, for all this,
When I shall tread upon the tyrant's head,
Or wear it on my sword, yet my poor country
Shall have more vices than it had before,
More suffer, and more sundry ways than ever, [30]
By him that shall succeed.

MACDUFF.

What should he be? [31]

MALCOLM.

It is myself I mean, in whom I know
All the particulars of vice so grafted [32]
That, when they shall be opened, black Macbeth [33]
Will seem as pure as snow, and the poor state
Esteem him as a lamb, being compared
With my confineless harms. [34]

---

25. absolute fear. complete mistrust
26. think. am mindful that
27. withal. in addition
28. right. claim to the throne
29. England. the King of England
30. more sundry. in more various
31. what. who
32. particulars. varieties. **grafted.** implanted
33. opened. unfolded (like a bud)
34. my confineless harms. unbounded evils

MACDUFF.

Not in the legions
Of horrid hell can come a devil more damned
In evils to top Macbeth. [35]

MALCOLM.

I grant him bloody,
Luxurious, avaricious, false, deceitful, [36]
Sudden, malicious, smacking of every sin [37]
That has a name. But there's no bottom, none,
In my voluptuousness. Your wives, your daughters,
Your matrons, and your maids could not fill up
The cistern of my lust, and my desire
All continent impediments would o'erbear [38]
That did oppose my will. Better Macbeth [39]
Than such an one to reign.

MACDUFF.

Boundless intemperance
In nature is a tyranny; it hath been [40]
Th' untimely emptying of the happy throne
And fall of many kings. But fear not yet [41]
To take upon you what is yours. You may
Convey your pleasures in a spacious plenty, [42]

---

35. **top.** surpass
36. **Luxurious.** lecherous
37. **Sudden.** violent
38. **continent impediments.** restraints
39. **will.** lust
40. **nature.** human nature
41. **yet.** nevertheless
42. **Convey.** manage with secrecy

And yet seem cold; the time you may so
   hoodwink. [43]
We have willing dames enough. There cannot be
That vulture in you to devour so many
As will to greatness dedicate themselves,
Finding it so inclined.

MALCOLM.

                          With this there grows
In my most ill-composed affection such [44]
A stanchless avarice that, were I king, [45]
I should cut off the nobles for their lands,
Desire his jewels and this other's house, [46]
And my more-having would be as a sauce
To make me hunger more, that I should forge [47]
Quarrels unjust against the good and loyal,
Destroying them for wealth.

MACDUFF.

                          This avarice
Sticks deeper, grows with more pernicious root
Than summer-seeming lust, and it hath been [48]
The sword of our slain kings. Yet do not fear; [49]
Scotland hath foisons to fill up your will [50]
Of your mere own. All these are portable, [51]

---

43. cold. chaste. **the time ... hoodwink** you may so fool
   the age. **hoodwink.** blindfold
44. ill-composed affection. evil character
45. stanchless. never-ending
46. his. one man's. **this other's.** another's
47. that. so that
48. summer-seeming. appropriate to youth
49. sword. cause of overthrow
50. foisons. plenty
51. Of ... own. in your own royal property alone.
   portable. bearable

With other graces weighed. [52]

MALCOLM.

But I have none. The king-becoming graces,
As justice, verity, temperance, stableness,
Bounty, perseverance, mercy, lowliness, [53]
Devotion, patience, courage, fortitude,
I have no relish of them, but abound [54]
In the division of each several crime, [55]
Acting it many ways. Nay, had I power, I should
Pour the sweet milk of concord into hell,
Uproar the universal peace, confound [56]
All unity on earth.

MACDUFF.

O Scotland, Scotland!

MALCOLM.

If such a one be fit to govern, speak.
I am as I have spoken.

MACDUFF.

Fit to govern?
No, not to live. O nation miserable,
With an untitled tyrant bloody-sceptered, [57]
When shalt thou see thy wholesome days again,
Since that the truest issue of thy throne
By his own interdiction stands accursed [58]
And does blaspheme his breed? Thy royal father [59]

---

52. weighed. balanced
53. lowliness. humility
54. relish. trace
55. division ... crime. variations of each kind of crime
56. Uproar. throw into an uproar
57. untitled. lacking rightful title
58. interdiction. exclusion
59. blaspheme. slander. **breed.** breeding

Was a most sainted king; the queen that bore thee,
Oft'ner upon her knees than on her feet,
Died every day she lived. Fare thee well. [60]
These evils thou repeat'st upon thyself
Hath banished me from Scotland. O my breast, [61]
Thy hope ends here!

MALCOLM.

Macduff, this noble passion,
Child of integrity, hath from my soul [62]
Wiped the black scruples, reconciled my thoughts
To thy good truth and honor. Devilish Macbeth
By many of these trains hath sought to win me [63]
Into his power, and modest wisdom plucks me [64]
From overcredulous haste. But God above
Deal between thee and me! For even now
I put myself to thy direction and
Unspeak mine own detraction, here abjure [65]
The taints and blames I laid upon myself
For strangers to my nature. I am yet [66]
Unknown to woman, never was forsworn, [67]
Scarcely have coveted what was mine own,
At no time broke my faith, would not betray
The devil to his fellow, and delight
No less in truth than life. My first false speaking
Was this upon myself. What I am truly [68]

---

60. **Died ... lived.**   prepared for heaven every day she lived
61. **breast.**   heart
62. **Child of integrity.**   a product of your integrity of spirit
63. **trains.**   plots
64. **modest ... me.**   wise prudence holds me back
65. **detraction.**   slander
66. **For.**   as
67. **Unknown to woman.**   a virgin

Is thine and my poor country's to command—
Whither indeed, before thy here-approach,
Old Siward with ten thousand warlike men,
Already at a point, was setting forth. [69]
Now we'll together; and the chance of goodness [70]
Be like our warranted quarrel! Why are you
  silent? [71]

MACDUFF.
Such welcome and unwelcome things at once
'Tis hard to reconcile.

[Enter a DOCTOR]

MALCOLM.
Well, more anon.—Comes the King forth, I pray
  you?

DOCTOR.
Ay, sir. There are a crew of wretched souls
That stay his cure. Their malady convinces [72]
The great assay of art; but at his touch— [73]
Such sanctity hath heaven given his hand—
They presently amend. [74]

MALCOLM.
               I thank you, Doctor.
                    [Exit DOCTOR]

---

68. **upon.** against
69. **at a point.** ready
70. **the chance of goodness.** may the chance of success
71. **Be ... quarrel.** be equal to the justice of our cause
72. **stay.** wait for. **convinces.** conquers
73. **assay of art.** efforts of medical skill
74. **presently.** immediately

MACDUFF.
What's the disease he means?
MALCOLM.
'Tis called the evil. [75]
A most miraculous work in this good king,
Which often, since my here-remain in England, [76]
I have seen him do. How he solicits heaven [77]
Himself best knows; but strangely-visited people, [78]
All swoll'n and ulcerous, pitiful to the eye,
The mere despair of surgery, he cures, [79]
Hanging a golden stamp about their necks [80]
Put on with holy prayers; and 'tis spoken,
To the succeeding royalty he leaves
The healing benediction. With this strange virtue [81]
He hath a heavenly gift of prophecy,
And sundry blessings hang about his throne
That speak him full of grace.

[*Enter* ROSS]

MACDUFF.
See who comes here.

MALCOLM.
My countryman, but yet I know him not. [82]

---

75. evil. scrofula (supposedly cured by the king's touch; James I claimed this power)
76. here-remain. stay
77. solicits. succeeds by prayer with
78. strangely-visited. afflicted by strange diseases
79. mere. complete
80. stamp. minted coin
81. virtue. healing power
82. My countryman. (Malcolm identifies him by his dress.)
   know. recognize

MACDUFF.

My ever-gentle cousin, welcome hither. [83]

MALCOLM.

I know him now. Good God, betimes remove [84]
The means that makes us strangers!

ROSS.

Sir, amen.

MACDUFF.

Stands Scotland where it did?

ROSS.

Alas, poor country,
Almost afraid to know itself. It cannot
Be called our mother, but our grave; where nothing [85]
But who knows nothing is once seen to smile; [86]
Where sighs and groans and shrieks that rend the
air
Are made, not marked; where violent sorrow seems [87]
A modern ecstasy. The dead man's knell [88]
Is there scarce asked for who, and good men's lives
Expire before the flowers in their caps,
Dying or ere they sicken. [89]

MACDUFF.

O, relation
Too nice, and yet too true! [90]

---

83. **gentle.** noble
84. **betimes.** quickly
85. **nothing.** no one
86. **But who.** except a person who. **once.** ever
87. **marked.** noticed
88. **modern ecstasy.** ordinary emotion
89. **or ere they sicken.** before they have had time to get sick.
90. **nice.** very accurate. **relation.** report

MALCOLM.

What's the newest grief?

ROSS.

That of an hour's age doth hiss the speaker; [91]
Each minute teems a new one. [92]

MACDUFF.

How does my wife?

ROSS.

Why, well.

MACDUFF.

And all my children?

ROSS.

Well too. [93]

MACDUFF.

The tyrant has not battered at their peace?

ROSS.

No, they were well at peace when I did leave 'em.

MACDUFF.

Be not a niggard of your speech. How goes 't?

ROSS.

When I came hither to transport the tidings
Which I have heavily borne, there ran a rumor [94]
Of many worthy fellows that were out, [95]

---

91. hiss. cause to be hissed (for repeating old news)
92. teems. teems with
93. well. (Ross cannot bring himself to give Macduff the bad news.)
94.heavily. sadly
95.out. in the field

Which was to my belief witnessed the rather [96]
For that I saw the tyrant's power afoot. [97]
Now is the time of help; your eye in Scotland
Would create soldiers, make our women fight,
To doff their dire distresses. [98]

MALCOLM.

Be 't their comfort
We are coming thither. Gracious England hath [99]
Lent us good Siward and ten thousand men;
An older and a better soldier none
That Christendom gives out. [100]

ROSS.

Would I could answer
This comfort with the like! But I have words
That would be howled out in the desert air,
Where hearing should not latch them. [101]

MACDUFF.

What concern they?
The general cause? Or is it a fee-grief [102]
Due to some single breast? [103]

ROSS.

No mind that's honest
But in it shares some woe, though the main part
Pertains to you alone.

---

96. **witnessed the rather.** made the more believable
97. **power.** army
98. **doff.** put off
99. **Gracious England.** Edward the Confessor
100. **gives out.** tells of
101. **latch.** catch
102. **fee-grief.** personal grief
103. **Due to.** owned by

MACDUFF.

If it be mine,
Keep it not from me; quickly let me have it.

ROSS.

Let not your ears despise my tongue forever,
Which shall possess them with the heaviest sound [104]
That ever yet they heard.

MACDUFF.

Hum! I guess at it.

ROSS.

Your castle is surprised, your wife and babes
Savagely slaughtered. To relate the manner
Were, on the quarry of these murdered deer, [105]
To add the death of you.

MALCOLM.

Merciful heaven!
What, man, ne'er pull your hat upon your brows; [106]
Give sorrow words. The grief that does not speak
Whispers the o'erfraught heart and bids it break. [107]

MACDUFF.

My children too?

ROSS.

Wife, children, servants, all
That could be found.

---

104. **possess them with.** put them in possession of
105. **quarry.** heap of slaughtered deer at a hunt
106. **pull your hat.** (a stage action indicating grief.)
107. **whispers.** whispers to. **o'erfraught.** overburdened

MACDUFF.

And I must be from thence! [108]

My wife killed too?

ROSS.

I have said.

MALCOLM.

Be comforted.
Let's make us medicines of our great revenge
To cure this deadly grief.

MACDUFF.

He has no children. All my pretty ones? [109]
Did you say all? O hell-kite! All?
What, all my pretty chickens and their dam
At one fell swoop? [110]

MALCOLM.

Dispute it like a man. [111]

MACDUFF.

I shall do so;
But I must also feel it as a man.
I cannot but remember such things were,
That were most precious to me. Did heaven look on
And would not take their part? Sinful Macduff,

---

108. **must.** had to
109. **He has no children.** no father would do such a thing;
(or, possibly,) since Macbeth has no children, there can
be no complete revenge
110. **fell swoop.** cruel swoop of the hell-kite, bird of prey
from hell
111. **Dispute it.** fight on the issue

They were all struck for thee! Naught that I am, [112]
Not for their own demerits, but for mine,
Fell slaughter on their souls. Heaven rest them now!

MALCOLM.
Be this the whetstone of your sword. Let grief
Convert to anger; blunt not the heart, enrage it.

MACDUFF.
O, I could play the woman with mine eyes
And braggart with my tongue! But, gentle heavens,
Cut short all intermission. Front to front [113]
Bring thou this fiend of Scotland and myself;
Within my sword's length set him. If he 'scape,
Heaven forgive him too!

MALCOLM.
This tune goes manly.
Come, go we to the King. Our power is ready; [114]
Our lack is nothing but our leave. Macbeth [115]
Is ripe for shaking, and the powers above
Put on their instruments. Receive what cheer you
    may. [116]
The night is long that never finds the day.

[Exit]

---

112. **for thee.** as punishment from God for your sins.
    Naught. wicked
113. **intermission.** delay. **Front to front.** face to face
114. **power.** army
115. **Our ... leave.** we need only to say farewell formally (to
    the English King)
116. **Put ... instruments.** set us on as their agents; or, arm
    themselves

---◆---

Synopsis of Act IV, Scene 3

This scene takes place in England in front of the palace of King Edward of England. Malcolm and Macduff enter, and Malcolm suggests that they go to some isolated place in the woods where they can weep without worrying about what people will think. Macduff says that he would rather fight against Macbeth and protect Scotland from the horrors and misery there. Malcolm says that he wonders where Macduff's loyalties are. He fears that Macduff will betray him to Macbeth. Macduff replies that he is not a double-crosser, but Malcolm adds that Macbeth is and that anyone associated with him is suspicious. Malcolm says that he cannot understand how Macduff could leave his wife and children unprotected with no word to them of where he has gone or why, unless he was sure Macbeth would not harm them. Macduff is deeply hurt by these remarks. He says he has only good intentions for Malcolm and Scotland and starts to leave. Malcolm detains him and says that he feels sure that he can get support for his claim to the Scottish throne with help from the English. Malcolm then describes his own character to Macduff and tells him that, although he is not a killer like Macbeth, he (Malcolm) has an even worse character than Macbeth in some ways. He describes his huge sexual appetite and says that no woman in Scotland would be safe if he were king. Malcolm then tells Macduff that he is incredibly greedy. He states that no man's property would be safe in Scotland if he were king. Finally,

Malcolm says that he lacks all the good qualities a king should have: justice, honesty, self-control, common sense, generosity, patience, courage, and strength. He is really interested in how to commit crimes. All this is too much for Macduff, who now says that he can never return to Scotland, which is doomed forever. Malcolm then tells him that his description of himself as an evil man was only a test of Macduff's loyalty. Malcolm says that he is in fact innocent and virtuous. His first lies, he says were those he just told to Macduff. At this point, Macduff does not know what to believe.

Just then, a Doctor enters, and Malcolm asks him if the king will be appearing. The Doctor replies that the king will come out to heal people ill with scrofula, a disease of the glands, thought to curable by the touch of King Edward, the Confessor, then King of England, and any king descended from him. Shakespeare may have written this scene to please King James I, who believed he had inherited this healing touch. Whether or not this is true, we are made aware of the contrast between Edward, a well-loved, peaceful king, and Macbeth, a murderous tyrant.

Ross enters. Macduff recognizes him, but Malcolm does not, perhaps because it has been so long since the two have seen one another. Macduff asks Ross what is happening is Scotland. Ross says that there is endless misery and death. When Malcolm asks his what the latest news is, Ross replies that bad news even an hour old would have been topped by worse news. Macduff asks about his wife and children, but at this point Ross cannot bring himself to tell Macduff what has happened.

Ross says that it is time to rebel against Macbeth.
All that is needed is a leader. Malcolm says that
England is sending an army of ten thousand men
under his uncle, Siward, the Earl of
Northumberland. Ross now turns to his terrible
news. Macduff senses that this news is for him,
and Ross begs him not to hate him for what he is
about to say. Ross then tells Macduff that his castle
has been invaded by Macbeth's men, who brutally
killed his wife and children. Macduff tries to hide
his weeping by pulling his hat down over his face.
Malcolm tells him say something, not to suffer
silently. Macduff, stunned, asks "My children too?"
Ross replies yes, wife, children, servants, everyone
who was trapped in the castle. Macduff, who still
does not want to believe what he hears, says "My
wife killed too?" Malcolm tries to tell him to change
his grief to revenge, and Macduff says that
Macbeth has no children. He blames himself for
his family's deaths. Finally he swears to kill
Macbeth personally. Malcolm tries again to rally
him, and says that the time has come to get rid of
Macbeth.

Before You Read Act V, Scene 1

This famous scene shows us what has happened to Lady Macbeth in the period since she was encouraging Macbeth to kill King Duncan. She is observed by her personal maid and a doctor. They cannot fully understand Lady Macbeth's strange behavior. We know, however, from what she says what her "illness" is. Notice whom she refers to in her speeches. What kind of "medical" advice does the doctor give the maid?

ACT V. Scene 1.

Location: Dunsinane. Macbeth's castle.

[*Enter a* DOCTOR OF PHYSIC *and a* WAITING-GENTLEWOMAN]

DOCTOR.
I have two nights watched with you, but can perceive no truth in your report. When was it she last walked?

GENTLEWOMAN.
Since His Majesty went into the field, I [1] have seen her rise from her bed, throw her nightgown upon her, unlock her closet [2], take forth paper, fold it, write upon 't, read it, afterwards seal it, and again return to bed; yet all this while in a most fast sleep.

DOCTOR.
A great perturbation in nature, to receive at once the benefit of sleep and do the effects of watching! [3] In this slumbery agitation [4], besides her walking and other actual performances, what, at any time, have you heard her say?

GENTLEWOMAN.
That, sir, which I will not report after her.

DOCTOR.
You may to me, and 'tis most meet you should.

---

1. **field.** battlefield
2. **closet.** chest
3. **effects of watching.** deeds of one awake
4. **agitation.** activity

GENTLEWOMAN.
Neither to you nor anyone, having no witness to confirm my speech.

[*Enter* LADY MACBETH, *with a taper*]

Lo you, here she comes! This is her very guise, and, upon my life, fast asleep. Observe her. Stand close. [5]

[*They stand aside*]

DOCTOR.
How came she by that light?

GENTLEWOMAN.
Why, it stood by her. She has light by her continually. 'Tis her command.

DOCTOR.
You see her eyes are open.

GENTLEWOMAN.
Ay, but their sense [6] are shut.

DOCTOR.
What is it she does now? Look how she rubs her hands.

GENTLEWOMAN.
It is an accustomed action with her to seem thus washing her hands. I have known her continue in this a quarter of an hour.

---

5. **close.** concealed
6. **sense.** powers of sight

LADY MACBETH.
Yet here's a spot.

DOCTOR.
Hark, she speaks. I will set down what comes from her, to satisfy [7] my remembrance the more strongly.

LADY MACBETH.
Out, damned spot! Out, I say! One —two —why then, 'tis time to do 't. Hell is murky. —Fie, my lord, fie, a soldier, and afeard? What need we fear who knows it, when none can call our power to account? Yet who would have thought the old man to have had so much blood in him?

DOCTOR.
Do you mark that?

LADY MACBETH.
The Thane of Fife had a wife. Where is she now? — What, will these hands ne'er be clean? —No more o' that, my lord, no more o' that; you mar all with this starting. [8]

DOCTOR.
Go to, go to. You have known what you should not.

GENTLEWOMAN.
She has spoke what she should not, I am sure of that. Heaven knows what she has known.

LADY MACBETH.
Here's the smell of the blood still. All the perfumes of Arabia will not sweeten this little hand. O, O, O!

---

7. **satisfy.** support
8. **this starting.** these startled movements

DOCTOR.
What a sigh is there! The heart is sorely charged. [9]

GENTLEWOMAN.
I would not have such a heart in my bosom for the dignity of the whole body. [10]

DOCTOR.
Well, well, well.

GENTLEWOMAN.
Pray God it be, sir.

DOCTOR.
This disease is beyond my practice. Yet I have known those which have walked in their sleep who have died holily in their beds.

LADY MACBETH.
Wash your hands, put on your nightgown; look not so pale! I tell you yet again, Banquo's buried. He cannot come out on 's grave. [11]

DOCTOR.
Even so?

LADY MACBETH.
To bed, to bed! There's knocking at the gate. Come, come, come, come, give me your hand. What's done cannot be undone. To bed, to bed, to bed!

[Exit LADY]

---

9. **sorely charged.** heavily burdened
10. **dignity.** worth
11. **on 's.** of his

DOCTOR.
Will she go now to bed?

GENTLEWOMAN.
Directly.

DOCTOR.
Foul whisperings are abroad. Unnatural deeds
Do breed unnatural troubles. Infected minds
To their deaf pillows will discharge their secrets.
More needs she the divine than the physician.
God, God forgive us all! Look after her;
Remove from her the means of all annoyance, [12]
And still keep eyes upon her. So, good night. [13]
My mind she has mated, and amazed my sight. [14]
I think, but dare not speak.

GENTLEWOMAN.
Good night, good Doctor.

[*Exit*]

---

12. **annoyance.** injury
13. **still.** constantly
14. **mated.** baffled

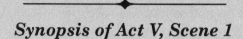

Synopsis of Act V, Scene 1

In the castle at Dunsinane, a Doctor and a Gentlewoman, a lady who personally serves Lady Macbeth, are talking about Lady Macbeth's strange behavior. The Doctor has been watching Lady Macbeth with this woman for two nights and doubts her stories of sleepwalking. She says that Lady Macbeth has been sleepwalking since Macbeth left for battle. She has seen Lady Macbeth rise, put on her nightgown, write something on paper, seal it, and return to bed, all while asleep. The Doctor wants to know if she has heard Lady Macbeth say anything during these sleepwalks. The woman refuses to repeat what she has heard. Lady Macbeth enters, carrying a lighted candle. Her eyes are open, but she sees nothing. She goes through the motions of washing her hands. She dreams that her hands are covered with blood that will not wash off. She refers to, but does not mention by name, not only King Duncan, whom she helped to kill, but Macduff's wife, who was killed by Macbeth's murderers. Thus, Lady Macbeth, who was so proud of her hard heart and who encouraged Macbeth to commit his first murders, is being driven mad by the very feelings she claimed not to have. The Doctor and the woman are frightened by Lady Macbeth's words. The Doctor says that Lady Macbeth's problems are not the kind that he can solve. They realize that Lady Macbeth and Macbeth must be guilty of many crimes. Lady Macbeth recalls her words to Macbeth when he saw Banquo's ghost. Banquo is buried, she said, and cannot rise from his grave. Then, imagining Macbeth is with her, she reaches for his hand and leads him to bed, saying sadly that what is done cannot be changed. The Doctor remarks that ugly rumors are circulating. Abnormal actions can produce abnormal worries, he says, and adds that Lady Macbeth has more need of a priest than a doctor. He tells the woman to keep anything dangerous away from Lady Macbeth and to watch her constantly. The Doctor says that he has suspicions that he dare not speak of.

————————◆————————

———————◆———————

Before You Read Act V, Scene 2

We learn in this scene that the struggle to overthrow Macbeth is already under way. Notice that Angus mentions a meeting near Birnam Wood. Where has this forest been mentioned before? Angus also says something about Macbeth's murders. What does this statement tell us?

———————◆———————

ACT V. Scene 2.

Location: The country near Dunsinane.

[*Drum and colors. Enter* MENTEITH,
CAITHNESS, ANGUS, LENNOX *and* SOLDIERS]

MENTEITH.
    The English power is near, led on by Malcolm,
    His uncle Siward, and the good Macduff.
    Revenges burn in them, for their dear causes [1]
    Would to the bleeding and the grim alarm [2]
    Excite the mortified man.

ANGUS.
                       Near Birnam Wood [3]
    Shall we well meet them; that way are they coming. [4]

CAITHNESS.
    Who knows if Donalbain be with his brother?

LENNOX.
    For certain, sir, he is not. I have a file [5]
    Of all the gentry. There is Siward's son,
    And many unrough youths that even now [6]
    Protest their first of manhood.

MENTEITH.
                  What does the tyrant? [7]

---

1. **dear.** strongly held
2. **bleeding.** bloody.   **alarm.** call to battle
3. **Excite ... man.** awaken the dead
4. **well.** no doubt
5. **file.** list
6. **unrough.** beardless
7. **protest.** assert

CAITHNESS.

Great Dunsinane he strongly fortifies.
Some say he's mad, others that lesser hate him
Do call it valiant fury; but for certain
He cannot buckle his distempered cause [8]
Within the belt of rule.

ANGUS.

Now does he feel
His secret murders sticking on his hands;
Now minutely revolts upbraid his faith-breach. [9]
Those he commands move only in command, [10]
Nothing in love. Now does he feel his title
Hang loose about him, like a giant's robe
Upon a dwarfish thief.

MENTEITH.

Who then shall blame
His pestered senses to recoil and start, [11]
When all that is within him does condemn
Itself for being there?

CAITHNESS.

Well, march we on
To give obedience where 'tis truly owed.
Meet we the medicine of the sickly weal, [12]

---

8. **distempered.** disease-swollen
9. **minutely ... faith-breach.** every minute a new revolt shows his lack of all trust and honor.
10. **in command.** under orders
11. **pestered.** tormented
12. **Meet we ... weal.** let us join forces with Malcolm, the physician of our sick land

And with him pour we in our country's purge
Each drop of us. [13]

LENNOX.

Or so much as it needs
To dew the sovereign flower and drown the weeds. [14]
Make we our march towards Birnam.

[Exit marching]

---

13. **Each ... us.** every last drop of our blood
14. **dew.** water.   **sovereign.** royal

Synopsis of Act V, Scene 2

In the countryside near Dunsinane, the Scottish nobles Menteith, Caithness, Angus, and Lennox enter with their soldiers. Menteith tells them that the English army is nearby, led by Malcolm, Siward, and Macduff, and all are eager to to do battle. Angus says that their forces will meet Malcolm's at Birnam Wood. Caithness asks if Donalbain will be with Malcolm. Lennox replies no, that he has seen a list of all the noblemen to be there. Many young men will be there, though, including Siward's son. Menteith asks what Macbeth is doing. Caithness replies that he is making his castle at Dunsinane ready for an attack. He also says that some think Macbeth has gone mad, others call his behavior wildly brave, but it is clear Macbeth is out of control. Angus says that Macbeth's secret murders are working against him, and that his only followers are those under his direct power. Menteith observes that Macbeth's conscience must be driving him crazy. Caithness tells them to continue on to the battle that will put Malcolm on the throne and restore sanity to Scotland.

---◆---

Before You Read Act V, Scene 3

In his castle at Dunsinane, things are going badly for Macbeth. He is angry at the thanes, the servants, and the court doctor, all for different reasons. As you read this scene, try to identify these reasons. Notice that Macbeth reassures himself with some information that he received earlier in the play.

---◆---

ACT V. Scene 3.

Location: Dunsinane. Macbeth's castle.

[*Enter MACBETH, DOCTOR, and ATTENDANTS*]

MACBETH.
Bring me no more reports. Let them fly all! [1]
Till Birnam wood remove to Dunsinane,
I cannot taint with fear. What's the boy Malcolm? [2]
Was he not born of woman? The spirits that know
All mortal consequences have pronounced me thus: [3]
"Fear not, Macbeth. No man that's born of woman
Shall e'er have power upon thee." Then fly, false
    thanes,
And mingle with the English epicures! [4]
The mind I sway by and the heart I bear [5]
Shall never sag with doubt nor shake with fear.

[*Enter SERVANT*]

The devil damn thee black, thou cream-faced loon! [6]
Where gott'st thou that goose look?

SERVANT.
There is ten thousand—

MACBETH.
                    Geese, villain?

---

1. **them.** the thanes. **fly.** desert
2. **taint with.** become infected with
3. **mortal consequences.** future human events
4. **epicures.** gluttons
5. **sway.** move
6. **loon.** stupid fellow

SERVANT.

Soldiers, sir.

MACBETH.

Go prick thy face and over-red thy fear, [7]
Thou lily-livered boy. What soldiers, patch.[8]
Death of thy soul! Those linen cheeks of thine [9]
Are counselors to fear. What soldiers, whey-face? [10]

SERVANT.
The English force, so please you.

MACBETH.
Take thy face hence. [Exit SERVANT] Seyton! —I
   am sick at heart
When I behold —Seyton, I say! —This push [11]
Will cheer me ever, or disseat me now. [12]
I have lived long enough. My way of life [13]
Is fall'n into the sere, the yellow leaf, [14]
And that which should accompany old age,
As honor, love, obedience, troops of friends, [15]
I must not look to have, but in their stead
Curses, not loud but deep, mouth-honor, breath,
Which the poor heart would fain deny and dare not.
Seyton!

---

7. **Go prick ... fear.** go prick or pinch your pale cheeks to
   bring some color into them
8. **patch.** fool
9. **of thy.** on your.   **linen.** pale as linen
10. **Are ... fear.** i.e., teach others to fear
11. **push.** effort
12. **disseat me.** take the throne away from me
13. **way.** course
14. **sere.** dry and withered condition
15. **As.** such as

[*Enter* SEYTON]

SEYTON.
What's your gracious pleasure?

MACBETH.
                              What news more?

SEYTON.
All is confirmed, my lord, which was reported.

MACBETH.
I'll fight till from my bones my flesh be hacked.
Give me my armor.

SEYTON.
                              'Tis not needed yet.

MACBETH.
I'll put it on.
Send out more horses. Skirr the country round. [16]
Hang those that talk of fear. Give me mine armor.
How does your patient, Doctor?

DOCTOR.
                              Not so sick, my lord,
As she is troubled with thick-coming fancies
That keep her from her rest.

MACBETH.
                              Cure her of that.
Canst thou not minister to a mind diseased,
Pluck from the memory a rooted sorrow,

---

16. **Skirr.** scour

Rase out the written troubles of the brain, [17]
And with some sweet oblivious antidote [18]
Cleanse the stuffed bosom of that perilous stuff [19]
Which weighs upon the heart?

DOCTOR.

Therein the patient
Must minister to himself.

MACBETH.
Throw physic to the dogs! I'll none of it. [20]
Come, put mine armor on. Give me my staff. [21]

[ATTENDANTS *arm him*]

Seyton, send out. Doctor, the thanes fly from me. —
Come, sir, dispatch. —If thou couldst, Doctor, cast [22]
The water of my land, find her disease, [23]
And purge it to a sound and pristine health, [24]
I would applaud thee to the very echo,
That should applaud again. —Pull 't off, I say. — [25]
What rhubarb, senna, or what purgative drug [26]
Would scour these English hence? Hear'st thou of
    them? [27]

---

17. **rase.** erase.   **written troubles of.** troubles written on
18. **oblivious.**   causing forgetfulness
19. **stuffed.**   clogged
20. **physic.**   medicine
21. **staff.**   baton symbolic of office
22. **dispatch.** hurry.   **cast.** diagnose
23. **water.**   urine, used in diagnosis
24. **purge.**   cleanse
25. **Pull 't off.**   pull off a piece of armor which has been put
    on incorrectly in Macbeth's haste
26. **senna.**   laxative
27. **scour.**   purge, cleanse

DOCTOR.

Ay, my good lord; your royal preparation
Makes us hear something.

MACBETH.

Bring it after me. — [28]
I will not be afraid of death and bane,
Till Birnam Forest came to Dunsinane.

[*Exit all but the* DOCTOR]

DOCTOR.

Were I from Dunsinane away and clear,
Profit again should hardly draw me here.

[*Exit*]

---

28. it. the armor that Macbeth has not yet put on

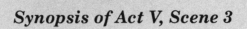

Synopsis of Act V, Scene 3

Macbeth enters a room in his castle at Dunsinane with the Doctor and some servants. Angrily, Macbeth tells the servants not to bring him any more reports about the thanes who are deserting him for the English side. It does not matter anyway, Macbeth tells them, because he has nothing to fear until Birnam Wood moves to Dunsinane. Also what has he to fear from Malcolm? Wasn't he born to a woman like other men? Another servant enters and informs Macbeth that an English army of ten thousand is advancing on Dunsinane. Macbeth is furious with him, and yells at him for looking afraid and causing fear among others at the castle. Macbeth tells him to get out and then calls on Seyton, a trusted servant. While he is waiting for Seyton, Macbeth reflects that he will never enjoy a normal old age with its honors, love, obedience, and crowds of friends. Instead he must put up with false courtesy and whispered curses. Seyton comes in and confirms the other servant's story about the English army. Macbeth demands his armor and starts putting it on. He asks the Doctor how Lady Macbeth is doing. The doctor says she is not physically sick but troubled with fears that prevent sleep. Macbeth says that these are what he wants the Doctor to get rid of. He wants to the Doctor to give her a drug that will relieve her of guilt and help her to forget the horrors she has seen. The Doctor tells him that, in cases such as this, the patient must cure herself. Then, says Macbeth, so much for medicine. Macbeth continues to struggle with his armor while he scolds the doctor. He asks the doctor what medicines would restore Scotland's good health and get rid of the English. The Doctor nervously replies that Macbeth's preparations for war seem like the right remedy. Macbeth leaves with half of his armor on. He repeats to Seyton, who follows Macbeth with the rest of the armor, that he has nothing to worry about until Birnam Wood moves to Dunsinane.

Before You Read Act V, Scene 4

The commanders of the English army meet near Birnam Wood. A startling plan of attack is put forth by Malcolm. Try to imagine the effect that hearing this plan would have on a live theater audience.

ACT V. Scene 4.

Location: Country near Birnam Wood.

[*Drum and colors. Enter* MALCOLM, SIWARD, MACDUFF, SIWARD'S SON, MENTEITH, CAITHNESS, ANGUS, LENNOX, ROSS, *and* SOLDIERS, *marching*]

MALCOLM.
Cousins, I hope the days are near at hand
That chambers will be safe.

MENTEITH.
                        We doubt it nothing. [1]

SIWARD.
What wood is this before us?

MENTEITH.
                        The wood of Birnam.

MALCOLM.
Let every soldier hew him down a bough
And bear 't before him. Thereby shall we shadow
The numbers of our host and make discovery [2]
Err in report of us.

SOLDIERS.
                        It shall be done.

SIWARD.
We learn no other but the confident tyrant

---

1. **chambers ... safe.** that people will be safe in their own
   homes. **nothing.** not at all
2. **discovery.** those who see us

Keeps still in Dunsinane and will endure [3]
Our setting down before 't. [4]

MALCOLM.

'Tis his main hope;
For where there is advantage to be given, [5]
Both more and less have given him the revolt, [6]
And none serve with him but constrain'e things
Whose hearts are absent too.

MACDUFF.

Let our just censures [7]
Attend the true event, and put we on
Industrious soldiership.

SIWARD.

The time approaches
That will with due decision make us know
What we shall say we have and what we owe. [8]
Thoughts speculative their unsure hopes relate,
But certain issue strokes must arbitrate— [9]
Towards which advance the war.[10]

[Exit, marching]

---

3. **Keeps.** remains. **endure.** allow
4. **setting down before.** laying siege to
5. **advantage.** opportunity
6. **more and less.** people of high and low rank
7. **Let ... event.** let true judgment await the actual outcome
8. **what ... owe.** what we only claim to have. **owe.** own
9. **Thoughts ... arbitrate.** guessing can only bring uncertain hopes; fighting must decide the actual outcome
10. **war.** army

---◆---

Synopsis of Act V, Scene 4

In the country near Birnam Wood, the invading English army assembles. Malcolm enters with Siward, Macduff, Siward's Son, Menteith, Caithness, and Angus. Malcolm tells them all that he hopes the time is near when people in Scotland will be safe in their own houses. He then tells the commanders to have every soldier cut a branch from a tree in the forest and carry it to conceal himself. This will make it impossible for Macbeth's forces to figure out how many soldiers there are in Malcolm's army. Siward says that Macbeth is prepared for an attack on his castle. Malcolm adds that people of all ranks are deserting Macbeth and that the only men fighting for him are those who are forced to. Macduff and Siward advise caution and agree that the battle will tell the true story.

---◆---

Before You Read Act V, Scene 5

In this important scene, Macbeth sees at last the beginning of his final destruction. He receives two pieces of terrible news. After hearing the first piece of news, Macbeth has a speech that shows Shakespeare at his peak as a poet. Read the speech carefully and notice the strong relationship between Macbeth's words and feelings.

ACT V. Scene 5.

Location: Dunsinane. Macbeth's castle.

[*Enter* MACBETH, SEYTON, *and* SOLDIERS, *with drum and colors*]

MACBETH.
Hang out our banners on the outward walls.
The cry is still, "They come!" Our castle's strength
Will laugh a siege to scorn. Here let them lie
Till famine and the ague eat them up. [1]
Were they not forced with those that should be
    ours, [2]
We might have met them dareful, beard to beard, [3]
And beat them backward home.
                    [*A cry within of women*]

                    What is that noise?

SEYTON.
It is the cry of women, my good lord.
                    [*He goes to the door*]

MACBETH.
I have almost forgot the taste of fears.
The time has been my senses would have cooled [4]
To hear a night-shriek, and my fell of hair [5]
Would at a dismal treatise rouse and stir [6]

---

1. **ague.** fever
2. **forced.** reinforced
3. **dareful.** boldly
4. **cooled.** felt the chill of terror
5. **my fell of hair.** the hair of my scalp
6. **dismal treatise.** scary story

As life were in 't. I have supped full with horrors; [7]
Direness, familiar to my slaughterous thoughts,
Cannot once start me.

[Seyton *returns*]

Wherefore was that cry? [8]

SEYTON.
The Queen, my lord, is dead.

MACBETH.
She should have died hereafter; [9]
There would have been a time for such a word.
Tomorrow, and tomorrow, and tomorrow
Creeps in this petty pace from day to day
To the last syllable of recorded time, [10]
And all our yesterdays have lighted fools
The way to dusty death. Out, out, brief candle! [11]
Life's but a walking shadow, a poor player
That struts and frets his hour upon the stage
And then is heard no more. It is a tale
Told by an idiot, full of sound and fury,
Signifying nothing.

[*Enter a* MESSENGER]

Thou com'st to use thy tongue; the story quickly.

---

7. **As.** as if
8. **start me.** make me start
9. **She ... hereafter.** she would have died someday
10. **recorded time.** the record of time
11. **dusty.** (God made man of dust, and at death he returns
   to dust.)

MESSENGER.

Gracious my lord,
I should report that which I say I saw,
But know not how to do 't.

MACBETH.

Well, say, sir.

MESSENGER.

As I did stand my watch upon the hill,
I looked toward Birnam, and anon, methought,
The wood began to move.

MACBETH.

Liar and slave!

MESSENGER.

Let me endure your wrath if 't be not so.
Within this three mile may you see it coming;
I say, a moving grove.

MACBETH.

If thou speak'st false,
Upon the next tree shall thou hang alive
Till famine cling thee. If thy speech be sooth, [12]
I care not if thou dost for me as much.
I pull in resolution, and begin [13]
To doubt th' equivocation of the fiend
That lies like truth. "Fear not, till Birnam Wood
Do come to Dunsinane," and now a wood
Comes toward Dunsinane. Arm, arm, and out!

---

12. **cling.** wither. **sooth.** truth
13. **pull in.** rein in

If this which he avouches does appear, [14]
There is nor flying hence nor tarrying here.
I 'gin to be aweary of the sun,
And wish th' estate o' the world were now undone. [15]
Ring the alarum bell! Blow wind, come wrack, [16]
At least we'll die with harness on our back. [17]

[*Exit*]

14. **avouches.** asserts
15. **estate.** settled order
16. **wrack.** ruin
17. **harness.** armor

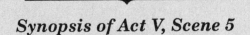

Synopsis of Act V, Scene 5

In the castle at Dunsinane, Macbeth talks to Seyton and some of his soldiers. He tells them that his castle is so strong that Malcolm's forces will never take it. They will starve and die of fever on the fields outside. Macbeth adds that if there were not so many Scottish defectors to Malcolm's forces, he could beat Malcolm's army in the field. His speech is interrupted by women's screams from somewhere in the castle. When Seyton runs out to see what has happened, Macbeth reflects that in former days he would have found screams in the night chilling. He adds that in those days his scalp would crawl when he heard a horrible story. Now, he has seen so much horror, he says, that nothing shocks him. Seyton returns and tells Macbeth that Lady Macbeth is dead. Macbeth, unmoved, says that she had to die sooner or later. In a brief speech, Macbeth says that the passing of time means nothing, life means nothing, death means nothing. Macbeth is already dead emotionally. A messenger enters and tells Macbeth that he and others have seen Birnam Wood moving! (What they have seen, of course, is Malcolm's men marching in the near darkness with their tree branches.) Macbeth, stunned, tells the messenger that he will be hanged if his news is untrue. He then begins to wonder about the motives of the vision which predicted no defeats for him until Birnam Wood moved to Dunsinane. Macbeth decides that he cannot wait in the castle for Malcolm's attack. As he tells his men to arm and follow him to the battlefield, he wishes for the end of the world.

———————◆———————

Before You Read Act V, Scene 6

Malcolm and his army arrive at Dunsinane. Notice the first thing that Malcolm tells them to do. Who will lead the first battle?

———————◆———————

ACT V. Scene 6.

Location: Dunsinane. Before Macbeth's castle.

[*Drum and colors. Enter* MALCOLM, SIWARD, MACDUFF, *and their army, with boughs*]

MALCOLM.
Now near enough. Your leafy screens throw down,
And show like those you are. You, worthy uncle, [1]
Shall with my cousin, your right noble son,
Lead our first battle. Worthy Macduff and we [2]
Shall take upon 's what else remains to do,
According to our order.

SIWARD.
                    Fare you well. [3]
Do we but find the tyrant's power tonight, [4]
Let us be beaten if we cannot fight.

MACDUFF.
Make all our trumpets speak! Give them all
     breath,
Those clamorous harbingers of blood and death. [5]

[*Exit. Alarums continued*]

---

1. **show.** appear
2. **battle.** battalion
3. **order.** plan of battle
4. **power.** army
5. **harbingers.** forerunners

Synopsis of Act V, Scene 6

In front of Macbeth's castle at Dunsinane, Malcolm enters with Siward, Macduff and the army, carrying their tree branches. Malcolm says that they are now close enough to the castle. He tells them to throw down the branches and show who they are. Reviewing their plans, he tells Siward and his son to lead the first battalion. He and Macduff will follow them up. Siward says farewell, and expresses the hope for a decisive fight. Macduff tells the trumpeters to call everyone to arms.

Before You Read Act V, Scene 7

The last two scenes of the play take place on the battlefield, with characters entering and exiting during the battle. In Scene 7, there is a fight between Macbeth and Siward's son. Notice Macbeth's final words to Young Siward. Macduff and Siward enter. Their exchange gives us some idea of how the battle is going. How do we know that Macbeth's army is losing?

ACT V. Scene 7.

Location: Before Macbeth's castle; the battle action is continuous here.

[*Enter* MACBETH]

MACBETH.
They have tied me to a stake. I cannot fly,
But bearlike I must fight the course. What's he [1]
That was not born of woman? Such a one
Am I to fear, or none.

[*Enter* YOUNG SIWARD]

YOUNG SIWARD.
What is thy name?

MACBETH.
Thou'lt be afraid to hear it.

YOUNG SIWARD.
No, though thou call'st thyself a hotter name
Than any is in hell.

MACBETH.
My name's Macbeth.

YOUNG SIWARD.
The devil himself could not pronounce a title
More hateful to mine ear.

MACBETH.
No, nor more fearful.

---

1.   **course.** round of bearbaiting, in which the bear was tied to a stake and dogs were set upon him

YOUNG SIWARD.
Thou liest, abhorrèd tyrant! With my sword
I'll prove the lie thou speak'st.

[Fight, *and* YOUNG SIWARD *slain*]

MACBETH.
Thou wast born of woman.
But swords I smile at, weapons laugh to scorn,
Brandished by man that's of a woman born.
[*Exit*]

[*Alarums. Enter* MACDUFF]

MACDUFF.
That way the noise is. Tyrant, show thy face!
If thou be'st slain, and with no stroke of mine,
My wife and children's ghosts will haunt me still.
I cannot strike at wretched kerns, whose arms [2]
Are hired to bear their staves. Either thou,
    Macbeth, [3]
Or else my sword with an unbattered edge
I sheathe again undeeded. There thou shouldst be; [4]
By this great clatter one of greatest note
Seems bruited. Let me find him, Fortune, [5]
And more I beg not.
[*Exit. Alarums*]

[*Enter* MALCOLM *and* SIWARD]

---

2. **kerns.** Irish foot soldiers; Macbeth is using the term
    here as an expression of contempt
3. **staves.** spears. **Either thou.** i.e., either I find you
4. **undeeded.** unused
5. **bruited.** reported

SIWARD.

This way, my lord. The castle's gently rendered: [6]
The tyrant's people on both sides do fight,
The noble thanes do bravely in the war,
The day almost itself professes yours,
And little is to do.

MALCOLM.

We have met with foes
That strike beside us.

SIWARD.

Enter, sir, the castle. [7]
[*Exit. Alarum*]

---

6.   **rendered.** surrendered
7.   **strike beside us.** miss us on purpose

Synopsis of Act V, Scene 7

Somewhere on the battlefield, Macbeth enters. He knows he is being defeated but determines to fight on to the end. He finds reassurance in the promise that he cannot be killed by any man born to a woman. Siward's son comes in and asks Macbeth's name. When Young Siward learns it is Macbeth, he challenges him. They fight, and Macbeth kills him. Macbeth observes, sarcastically, that Young Siward was born to a woman. He does not fear swords and weapons used by men born to women, he repeats as he leaves. Macduff comes in. He is only interested in killing Macbeth and avenging the murders of his wife and children. He runs off in pursuit of Macbeth. Siward and Malcolm enter. Siward tells Malcolm that Macbeth's castle has been easily captured. He says that Macbeth's men are fighting among themselves. Malcolm's men have fought bravely, he adds, and the battle is almost won. Malcolm says that he has fought with men on the other side who deliberately miss him with their swords. They enter the castle.

———————◆———————

Before You Read Act V, Scene 8

In this final scene of the play, Macduff finds
Macbeth on the battlefield. As they fight, Macbeth
finally discovers that the powers of darkness have
betrayed him, as Banquo said they might after the
Witches appeared to both of them. Notice the trick
they have played on Macbeth. How does he react
when he finds out? Malcolm, Siward, and Ross
come in, and Siward finds out about the death of
his son. Is Siward's reaction believable?

———————◆———————

ACT V. Scene 8.

Location: Before Macbeth's castle, as the battle continues.

[*Enter* MACBETH]

MACBETH.
Why should I play the Roman fool and die [1]
On mine own sword? whiles I see lives, the gashes [2]
Do better upon them.

[*Enter* MACDUFF]

MACDUFF.
                    Turn, hellhound, turn!

MACBETH.
Of all men else I have avoided thee.
But get thee back. My soul is too much charged
With blood of thine already.

MACDUFF.
                        I have no words;
My voice is in my sword, thou bloodier villain
Than terms can give thee out! [3]

                        [*Fight. Alarum*]

---

1. **play ... die.** commit suicide, like Brutus, Mark Antony, and others in the moment of defeat
2. **Whiles ... lives.** as long as I see any enemy living
3. **give thee out.** describe you

MACBETH.
                                    Thou losest labor.
As easy mayst thou the intrenchant air [4]
With thy keen sword impress as make me bleed. [5]
Let fall thy blade on vulnerable crests;
I bear a charmèd life, which must not yield
To one of woman born.

MACDUFF.
                          Despair thy charm, [6]
And let the angel whom thou still hast served [7]
Tell thee, Macduff was from his mother's womb
Untimely ripped. [8]

MACBETH.
Accursèd be that tongue that tells me so,
For it hath cowed my better part of man! [9]
And be these juggling friends no more believed [10]
That palter with us in a double sense, [11]
That keep the word of promise to our ear
And break it to our hope. I'll not fight with thee.

MACDUFF.
Then yield thee, coward,
And live to be the show and gaze o' the time! [12]

---

4. **intrenchant.** that cannot be cut
5. **impress.** make a dent in
6. **Despair.** despair of
7. **angel.** evil angel, Macbeth's genius. **still.** always
8. **Untimely.** prematurely
9. **better ... man.** courage
10. **juggling.** deceiving
11. **palter ... sense.** tell us things that can have two meanings
12. **gaze o' the time.** spectacle of the age

We'll have thee, as our rarer monsters are, [13]
Painted upon a pole, and underwrit, [14]
"Here may you see the tyrant."

MACBETH.

I will not yield
To kiss the ground before young Malcolm's feet
And to be baited with the rabble's curse.
Though Birnam Wood be come to Dunsinane,
And thou opposed, being of no woman born,
Yet I will try the last. Before my body [15]
I throw my warlike shield. Lay on, Macduff,
And damned be him that first cries, "Hold,
    enough!"

[Exit, fighting. Alarums]

[Enter fighting, and MACBETH *slain. Exit* MAC-
DUFF *with* MACBETH'S *body. Retreat, and
flourish. Enter, with drum and colors,*
MALCOLM, SIWARD, ROSS, THANES, *and* SOL-
DIERS]

MALCOLM.
I would the friends we miss were safe arrived.

SIWARD.
Some must go off; and yet, by these I see [16]
So great a day as this is cheaply bought.

---

13. **monsters.** freaks
14. **Painted ... pole.** i.e., painted on a board hung on a pole
15. **the last.** my last resort
16. **go off.** die. **by these.** to judge by these here

MALCOLM.
Macduff is missing, and your noble son.

ROSS.
Your son, my lord, has paid a soldier's debt.
He only lived but till he was a man,
The which no sooner had his prowess confirmed
In the unshrinking station where he fought, [17]
But like a man he died.

SIWARD.
                    Then he is dead?

ROSS.
Ay, and brought off the field. Your cause of sorrow
Must not be measured by his worth, for then
It hath no end.

SIWARD.
                    Had he his hurts before?

ROSS.
Ay, on the front.

SIWARD.
                    Why then, God's soldier be he!
Had I as many sons as I have hairs
I would not wish them to a fairer death.
And so, his knell is knolled.

MALCOLM.
                    He's worth more sorrow,
And that I'll spend for him.

---

17. **unshrinking station.** place from which he did not back
    off

SIWARD.

He's worth no more.
They say he parted well and paid his score, [18]
And so, God be with him! Here comes newer comfort.

[*Enter* MACDUFF, *with* MACBETH'S *head*]

MACDUFF.

Hail, King! For so thou art. Behold where stands [19]
Th' usurper's cursèd head. The time is free. [20]
I see thee compassed with thy kingdom's pearl, [21]
That speak my salutation in their minds,
Whose voices I desire aloud with mine:
Hail, King of Scotland!

ALL.

Hail, King of Scotland!

[*Flourish*]

MALCOLM.

We shall not spend a large expense of time
Before we reckon with your several loves [22]
And make us even with you. My thanes and kinsmen, [23]

---

18. **parted.** departed.   **score.** reckoning
19. **stands.** on a pole
20. **The ... free.** Our country is free
21. **compassed ... pearl.** surrounded by the noblest people in your kingdom
22. **reckon ... loves.** reward each of you for your devotion
23. **make ... you.** repay your worthiness

Henceforth be earls, the first that ever Scotland
In such an honor named.   What's more to do
Which would be planted newly with the time, [24]
As calling home our exiled friends abroad
That fled the snares of watchful tyranny,
Producing forth the cruel ministers [25]
Of this dead butcher and his fiendlike queen—
Who, as 'tis thought, by self and violent hands [26]
Took off her life—this, and what needful else
That calls upon us, by the grace of Grace
We will perform in measure, time, and place. [27]
So, thanks to all at once and to each one,
Whom we invite to see us crowned at Scone.

[*Flourish. Exit all*]

---

24. **would ... time.** should be done at the beginning of this
    new age
25. **Producing forth.** bringing forward to trial.
    ministers. agents
26. **self and violent.** her own violent
27. **in measure ... place.** fittingly at the appropriate time
    and place

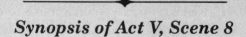

Synopsis of Act V, Scene 8

In another part of the battlefield, Macbeth enters and says that he will not consider suicide. As long as other men are living, it is better to kill them. Macduff comes in behind Macbeth and commands him to turn around. Macbeth tells him to go away. He says that he has avoided Macduff because he has killed too many of Macduff's family already. Macduff is not interested in talking. He begins to fight Macbeth. Macbeth tells Macduff that he might as well be waving his sword in the air because he is magically protected from any man born to a woman. Macduff tells Macbeth not to put any hope in this magic. He then reveals to Macbeth that his mother died before he was born. He was not born, he was torn from his mother's body. Macbeth curses Macduff and the devils who have tricked him with wordplay. He refuses to fight Macduff. Macduff tells Macbeth that if he gives up, he will be exhibited like a freak at a fair and ridiculed and despised for life. Macbeth replies that he will not give up. He will not recognize Malcolm as king. He will not be exhibited to the crowds as a freak. Even though Birnam Wood has come to Dunsinane and Macduff was not born to a woman, he will fight on with all the strength and courage he has left. The two men move out of sight as they fight. As they become visible again, Macduff has won the fight and Macbeth dies. Macduff goes off with Macbeth's body. Malcolm, Siward, Ross, the other thanes and soldiers enter. Malcolm says that they have lost some friends in the battle. Siward answers that, as battles go, not too many men have been lost. Malcolm reminds Siward that his own son and Macduff are still missing. Ross then tells Siward that his son is dead. He adds that Young Siward died bravely. Siward asks if his son's wounds were on the front of his body (in other words, did he die facing his enemy). Ross replies that he did. Siward says he could not wish for a more noble death for his son. Malcolm promises to hold a lavish funeral for him, but Siward says no, that God will reward his son for his bravery. Macduff enters, carrying Macbeth's head. He congratulates Malcolm, who is supported by Scotland's finest men, and calls on them to acclaim Malcolm King of Scotland. Malcolm accepts and gives the thanes and his relatives the title of earl, the first time the title has been used in Scotland. He goes on to say that his next act as king will be to ask all the Scots who have fled Scotland during Macbeth's reign to come home. He calls the dead Macbeth a butcher and compares Lady Macbeth to a fiend. He adds that she probably killed herself. He continues by saying that the exiled Scots will be asked back at the right time and place. Malcolm thanks the assembled noblemen and soldiers and invites them to his coronation at Scone.

REVIEWING

YOUR

READING

Act I, Scene 1

FINDING THE MAIN IDEA

1. The main purpose of this scene is to
   (A) show us what witches look like (B) establish a mood of evil (C) introduce us to a cat and a toad (D) tell us what will happen to Macbeth.

REMEMBERING DETAILS

2. What is Greymalkin?
   (A) the Third Witch (B) another name for hurlyburly (C) the place where the witches will meet (D) the First Witch's helper

DRAWING CONCLUSIONS

3. What do the witches mean when they say "Fair is foul, and foul is fair"?
   (A) the weather is both bad and good (B) we are both mean and ugly (C) we like evil better than good (D) thunder and lightning always go together

IDENTIFY THE MOOD

4. Shakespeare placed this scene at the beginning of *Macbeth* to
   (A) create an interest in the weather (B) create a sense of evil things to come (C) cause curiosity about where the witches came from (D) avoid introducing too many characters at once.

THINKING IT OVER

The witches in this scene have a certain power that most witches do not have. What is it? Give examples of this power.

Act I, Scene 2

FINDING THE MAIN IDEA

1. The main purpose of this scene is to
   (A) show how bloody battles were in eleventh-century Scotland (B) introduce King Duncan (C) show us how everyone feels about Macbeth (D) show that Macbeth is better than Banquo.

REMEMBERING DETAILS

2. Macdonwald is
   (A) a captain in King Duncan's army (B) a rebel from Ireland (C) the Thane of Cawdor (D) the King of Sweden

3. Where does Macbeth defeat Sweno?
   (A) Forres (B) Norway (C) Fife (D) Cawdor

DRAWING CONCLUSIONS

4. What does King Duncan mean when he says to the Captain "So well thy words become thee as thy wounds; They smack of honor both"?
   (A) Having told me what I want to hear, you can die happy. (B) You are bleeding badly, and you should see a doctor. (C) Both your news and your wounds tell me that you are a brave man. (D) Judging from your wounds, you had better stick to speeches and leave the fighting to other men.

USING YOUR REASON

5. King Duncan gives Macbeth the title of Thane of Cawdor because
   (A) Macbeth loves to kill (B) he hears that Macbeth is brave and clever in battle (C) he admires Macbeth's morals (D) he wants to prevent Banquo from getting the title.

THINKING IT OVER

Based on the information he hears in this scene, does King Duncan have any reason not to trust Macbeth?

Act I, Scene 3

REMEMBERING DETAILS

1. Since the three witches' last meeting, the First Witch has been
   (A) killing pigs (B) planning her revenge on a sailor's wife (C) getting the other witches ready for their meeting with Macbeth (D) planning a sea voyage.
2. At the beginning of this scene Macbeth is
   (A) Thane of Glamis (B) Thane of Cawdor (C) Sinel (D) none of the above.
3. When the witches appear to Macbeth and Banquo, they
   (A) speak only when they are told to (B) start talking at once (C) make fun of Banquo (D) tell Macbeth what to do next.
4. When the witches call Macbeth Thane of Cawdor, the former Thane of Cawdor
   (A) has been executed (B) has been banished from Scotland (C) is still alive in Scotland (D) is in prison.

DRAWING CONCLUSIONS

5. When Macbeth asks Banquo "Do you not hope your children shall be kings, When those that gave the Thane of Cawdor to me Promised no less to them?" Banquo's reaction
   (A) shows that he does not want to encourage Macbeth's hopes to be king (B) shows that he does not believe anything the witches have said (C) shows that he is envious of Macbeth (D) shows that he does not trust Macbeth.
6. When Banquo warns Macbeth: "But 'tis strange: And oftentimes, to win us to our harm, The instruments of darkness tell us truths, Win us with honest trifles, to betray's In deepest consequence," Macbeth
   (A) is shocked and worried (B) realizes that Banquo wants to be king (C) ignores the warning (D) wonders when the witches will appear again.

USING YOUR REASON

7. It seems likely that the witches are real rather than imaginary because
(A) Banquo clearly describes them (B) both Banquo and Macbeth can see them (C) the witches can foretell the future (D) they speak English like the other characters.

8. Macbeth is both happy and upset when Ross tells him that he has been made Thane of Cawdor because
(A) he is sorry that the former Thane of Cawdor is a traitor (B) he wanted another title (C) he is worried about how he will become king (D) Banquo did not get a title.

THINKING IT OVER

1. Macbeth's first words in the play, "So foul and fair a day I have not seen," echo words the witches said earlier. His words have an obvious, factual meaning. They also have a deeper, more important meaning. Explain both.

2. At the end of this scene, what has Macbeth decided to do about becoming king? Quote a line or two to justify your answer.

Act I, Scene 4

FINDING THE MAIN IDEA

1. Macbeth knows he must kill to become king when
(A) he hears that the former Thane of Cawdor has been executed (B) Duncan says he likes Banquo as much as he likes Macbeth (C) he hears that Duncan will be coming to his castle (D) Duncan chooses Malcolm to follow him as king.

REMEMBERING DETAILS

2. In this scene, the title Prince of Cumberland is given to
(A) Banquo (B) Malcolm (C) Macbeth (D) Ross

3. Malcolm describes to the king
(A) Macbeth's bravery on the battlefield (B) the Prince of Cumberland's trip to Inverness (C) the execution of the Thane of Cawdor (D) his brother Donalbain.

DRAWING CONCLUSIONS

4. When Malcolm says of the Thane of Cawdor that "...nothing in his life Became him like the leaving it" he means that
(A) the last moments of Cawdor's life were his finest
(B) everyone was relieved to see him executed (C) the king was lucky to miss the execution (D) traitors should always be executed.

USING YOUR REASON

5. When Macbeth speaks of the "step On which I must fall down, or else o'erleap, For in my way it lies" he is referring to
(A) the staircase leading out of the palace (B) Duncan's naming Malcolm as Prince of Cumberland (C) Duncan's liking for Banquo (D) Duncan's visit to Inverness.

THINKING IT OVER

Why is King Duncan's remark that "there's no art To find the mind's construction in the face" so appropriate in this scene?

Act I, Scene 5

FINDING THE MAIN IDEA

1. It is Lady Macbeth who
(A) sends a letter to Macbeth (B) plans the banquet dinner for King Duncan (C) first suggests that Macbeth kill the king (D) is too kind to consider killing anyone

REMEMBERING DETAILS

2. Macbeth informs Lady Macbeth in his letter
(A) that King Duncan is about to arrive at their castle
(B) of the news he received from the witches (C) of his thoughts about killing the king (D) of their upcoming wedding anniversary.

3. Lady Macbeth knows that she and Macbeth must murder Duncan on the night that he arrives at their castle because
(A) Duncan will be alone with them (B) they can blame the murder on Banquo (C) they can get everybody drunk at the dinner (D) Duncan plans to stay only one night.

DRAWING CONCLUSIONS

4. When Lady Macbeth says of Macbeth, "Yet I do fear thy nature; It is too full o' th' milk of human kindness To catch the nearest way," she means (A) she is afraid that he will want to murder her instead of the king (B) she is worried because Macbeth's responsible nature will prevent him from acting (C) she knows that Macbeth would never do anything that involved killing (D) she fears that Macbeth will blame her if she persuades him to kill Duncan.

5. Lady Macbeth tells Macbeth to "put This night's great business into my dispatch." She is referring to (A) the big banquet they are planning for Duncan (B) winning Duncan's favor for themselves (C) her plans to murder Duncan (D) finding rooms in their castle for the guests.

USING YOUR REASON

6. Why does Lady Macbeth call on the forces of darkness to "unsex" her? (A) She fears that, as a woman, she may not be tough enough to go through with the murder. (B) She wants to call up more supernatural beings like the witches. (C) She is thinking of becoming a nun. (D) She plans to be as masculine as Macbeth so he will do what she says.

7. We can assume from Macbeth's last words to Lady Macbeth in this scene ("We will speak further.") that (A) he agrees with everything Lady Macbeth says (B) he has more important things to do than listen to Lady Macbeth (C) he has not yet decided to go through with the murder (D) he is needed somewhere else in the castle.

THINKING IT OVER

In Shakespeare's time, men and women were thought to have very different qualities. How do you think Lady Macbeth views herself as a woman? What "male" qualities does she feel she lacks?

Act I, Scene 6

FINDING THE MAIN IDEA

1. It is clear from what King Duncan says in this scene that
(A) he prefers the outdoors to the indoors   (B) he is
already suspicious of Lady Macbeth   (C) he has no idea
of what Macbeth and his wife are really planning for him
(D) he prefers Macbeth to Lady Macbeth.

REMEMBERING DETAILS

2. When Duncan asks where Macbeth is, Duncan
(A) knows he is somewhere in the castle   (B) fears that
Macbeth got lost on the ride to Dunsinane   (C) is worried
about whether the Macbeths are expecting him
(D) is merely being polite.

DRAWING CONCLUSIONS

3. At the end of the scene, King Duncan says to Lady
Macbeth of Macbeth, "We love him highly, And shall continue our graces towards him." By *graces,* he probably
means
(A) polite behavior   (B) favors   (C) appointments to military duty   (D) visits to Dunsinane.

IDENTIFY THE MOOD

4. The mood is this scene is very pleasant. The King and
Banquo comment on the beautiful scenery and weather,
and everyone is very polite. Shakespeare probably wrote
the scene this way
(A) to show how life really was in eleventh-century
Scotland   (B) to show how stupid most kings are
(C) to set us up for the horror to come   (D) to show that
Lady Macbeth has a good side as well as a bad side.

THINKING IT OVER

Based on what happens in this scene, can you see any
reason why King Duncan should have been more
cautious about Macbeth's invitation?

Act I, Scene 7

FINDING THE MAIN IDEA

1. Without the influence of Lady Macbeth, it is likely that Macbeth
   (A) might never have killed Duncan   (B) would have been content to remain Thane of Cawdor   (C) would never have won the battle for Scotland   (D) would have turned down the crown in favor of Malcolm.

2. We can assume from Macbeth's first speech in this scene that he
   (A) makes quick decisions   (B) does not believe in heaven and hell   (C) cannot stand Lady Macbeth
   (D) none of the above.

DRAWING CONCLUSIONS

3. Macbeth tells Lady Macbeth that they should not go through with their plans to kill Duncan. He tells her that he has "bought Golden opinions from all sorts of people, Which would be worn now in their newest gloss, Not cast aside so soon." He is saying that he
   (A) is making more money than ever before and does not want to endanger his income   (B) has a wonderful reputation at the moment and wants to keep and enjoy it
   (C) has found some witches who can foretell the future and he plans to use them   (D) knows all sorts of people who he can get to commit the murder.

4. Why does Macbeth tell Lady Macbeth to "Bring forth men-children only; For thy undaunted mettle should compose Nothing but males"?
   (A) She has planned the murder so well   (B) She has shown that she can be ruthless and cold-blooded
   (C) She believes in going after what she wants
   (D) all of the above.

USING YOUR REASON

5. Although we do not know when it happened, we can probably assume from Lady Macbeth's question to Macbeth: "What beast was 't then That made you break this enterprise to me?"
(A) that she has heard about the gray cat and the toad
(B) that she thinks Macbeth has been lying to her
(C) that Macbeth may have been the first to suggest that they get rid of Duncan   (D) none of the above.

THINKING IT OVER

Macbeth and Lady Macbeth have no children. Give some reasons, based on their conversation is this scene, why this is so.

Act II, Scene 1

FINDING THE MAIN IDEA

1. By the end of this scene, we know that Macbeth
(A) now hopes that Lady Macbeth will murder Duncan
(B) is more worried about Banquo than anything else
(C) is losing his mind   (D) is resolved to murder Duncan but is still troubled about it.

REMEMBERING DETAILS

2. Banquo tells Fleance that he cannot sleep because of bad dreams. We find out later that he is dreaming about
(A) the meeting with the three witches   (B) the upcoming banquet for Duncan   (C) the terrible battle he and Macbeth have just won   (D) possible harm coming to Fleance.

DRAWING CONCLUSIONS

3. During the vision of the dagger, Macbeth says "I see thee yet, in form as palpable As this which now I draw." He is
(A) quickly making a drawing of the vision so he will not forget it   (B) drawing away from the vision   (C) admitting that he cannot make up his mind   (D) drawing his own dagger.

4. Macbeth says of the vision of the dagger, "There's no such thing. It is the bloody business which informs Thus to mine eyes." What does Macbeth mean by "bloody business"?
(A) the drops of blood on the dagger (B) the plans for the murder (C) the predictions of the witches (D) none of the above.

USING YOUR REASON
5. A bell rings at the end of Macbeth's speech, and he says, "Hear it not, Duncan, for it is a knell That summons thee to heaven, or to hell." What he means is
(A) I hope the bell does not wake you up, because it will be easier for me to kill you when you are asleep
(B) Since I do not know the state of your soul at the moment, I cannot say whether you will go to heaven or hell (C) It will be a mercy for you not to know when you are about to be killed (D) all of the above.

THINKING IT OVER
Macbeth concludes his long speech by saying that words are no substitute for acts. Why is this a turning point in the play?

Act II, Scene 2

FINDING THE MAIN IDEA
1. Macbeth has brought himself to murder Duncan, but
(A) he still wishes Lady Macbeth had done it
(B) he cannot remember what happened in Duncan's room (C) he is horrified by what he has done
(D) he does not want to talk about it.

REMEMBERING DETAILS
2. What was it that Macbeth wanted to do in the king's bedroom that he could not do?
(A) answer the Duncan's sons' blessing with an "amen"
(B) kill the guards (C) kill Malcolm and Donalbain
(D) strangle Duncan rather than stab him.

3. What was it that Macbeth was supposed to do in the king's bedroom that he could not do?
(A) leave a suicide note forged in Duncan's handwriting (B) plant the murder weapons on the guards (C) kill Malcolm and Donalbain (D) try to clean up as much blood as possible.

DRAWING CONCLUSIONS

4. When Macbeth thinks he hears a voice saying "Macbeth shall sleep no more," he fears that
(A) someone has witnessed the murder (B) he will not live to go to bed again (C) guilt will prevent him from ever sleeping well again (D) one of Duncan's sons has awakened.
5. According to Lady Macbeth, "The sleeping and the dead Are but pictures. 'Tis the eye of childhood That fears a painted devil." She is telling Macbeth that
(A) only children are afraid of sleeping people and dead bodies (B) he is imagining too many things (C) sleepers and dead bodies have no souls (D) children are afraid of devils and they ought to be.

USING YOUR REASON

6. Judging from Lady Macbeth's remarks to Macbeth, such as "Consider it not so deeply" and "Infirm of purpose!," we can see that
(A) she agrees with everything he says (B) she is not interested in what he says (C) she is annoyed by his fear and guilt (D) she knows he acts funny after he kills.
7. In her remark to Macbeth, "My hands are of your color, but I shame To wear a heart so white," Lady Macbeth is saying
(A) fear has drained all her blood to the lower part of her body (B) she is as guilty as he and sorry she did not actually kill Duncan (C) she and Macbeth have hands the same color but elsewhere her skin is lighter (D) she looks the same as Macbeth, but his blood is redder than hers.

8. What excuse does Lady Macbeth give for not killing Duncan herself?
(A) as a woman she might not be physically strong enough to do it   (B) it is harder to clean blood off women's clothes   (C) she does the thinking, Macbeth does the killing   (D) none of the above.

THINKING IT OVER
1. The most important events in this scene, especially the murder, take place off stage. Why did Shakespeare write the scene this way?
2. At the end of the previous scene, Macbeth hears a bell and thinks of Duncan. At the end of this scene, he hears a knocking and thinks of Duncan again. How has his view of the King changed?

Act II, Scene 3

FINDING THE MAIN IDEA
1. At the end of this scene, Macbeth and Lady Macbeth
(A) have pinned the blame for Duncan's murder on Malcolm and Donalbain   (B) are already planning more murders   (C) seem to have gotten away with murdering Duncan   (D) are named King and Queen of Scotland.
2. The murder of Duncan is viewed by Macduff, Lennox, and Banquo as
(A) unbelievably horrible   (B) the kind of thing that happens in eleventh-century Scotland   (C) the fault of Macbeth and Lady Macbeth   (D) none of the above

REMEMBERING DETAILS
3. The murder of Duncan is first discovered by
(A) Lennox   (B) Macduff   (C) Malcolm   (D) the porter.
4. The first reaction of Duncan's two sons, Malcolm and Donalbain, to their father's murder is
(A) great relief   (B) sorrow and weeping   (C) fainting   (D) to get away quickly.

DRAWING CONCLUSIONS

5. When Macbeth says, "Had I but died an hour before this chance, I had lived a blessed time; for from this instant There's nothing serious in mortality," he is
(A) expressing his regret over killing Duncan (B) saying that the murder of Duncan will make people forget his military victories (C) talking to himself as usual (D) pretending to be surprised by Duncan's murder.

6. As he is about to leave for Ireland, Donalbain tells Malcolm that at Inverness "There's daggers in men's smiles...." He is saying
(A) he cannot take another evil grin (B) you cannot trust anyone around here (C) he's seen Macbeth kill with a smile on his face (D) the people here are "armed to the teeth."

USING YOUR REASON

7. Judging from Malcolm and Donalbain's behavior in this scene, it is probable that they
(A) know Macbeth killed Duncan (B) know the guards did not kill Duncan (C) know they must raise armies elsewhere (D) know they may be next on the murderer's killing list.

8. Macbeth claims he killed the guards because
(A) he loved the king so much (B) they were covered with blood (C) he was angry and acted unthinkingly (D) all of the above.

IDENTIFY THE MOOD

9. At the beginning of this scene, Lennox reports all sorts of strange happenings. Which of the following doesn't he mention?
(A) earthquakes (B) owls screeching (C) chimneys being blown down (D) witches flying about.

10. It is possible to see this early in the play that Macbeth and his evil acts are associated with
(A) being a Scot (B) Inverness (C) night (D) bells ringing and porters knocking.

THINKING IT OVER

Looking over the reactions of all the characters to King Duncan's murder, can you say that anyone clearly suspects Macbeth?

Act II, Scene 4

FINDING THE MAIN IDEA

1. Ross and the old man believe that the evil doings in Macbeth's castle
   (A) are reflected in nature   (B) could only happen in Scotland   (C) are Macbeth's fault   (D) mean that witches are nearby.

REMEMBERING DETAILS

2. Judging from Ross's first remarks, this scene takes place
   (A) around 2:00 A.M.   (B) at breakfast time   (C) at the same time as the murder   (D) just before daybreak.

DRAWING CONCLUSIONS

3. The old man says that " ... this sore night Hath trifled former knowings." He means
   (A) he is so shocked he has forgotten everything
   (B) he slept badly because he was so sore   (C) he has never seen such a night before   (D) he knows things he cannot tell Ross

USING YOUR REASON

4. Macduff suspects Macolm and Donalbain bribed the guards to kill Duncan because
   (A) they hated their father   (B) he is sure Macbeth could not have done it   (C) their bedroom was next to Duncan's   (D) none of the above.

IDENTIFY THE MOOD

5. Shakespeare clearly wanted to establish a connection in Macbeth between evil, Macbeth, and
   (A) animals   (B) night   (C) Scotland   (D) the throne of Scotland.

Act III, Scene 1

FINDING THE MAIN IDEA
1. Macbeth decides he must kill Banquo because
   (A) Banquo was the only other person who saw the
   witches   (B) he is jealous of Banquo's popularity among
   the other thanes   (C) he resents the fact that Banquo's
   descendents will be kings and not his   (D) having gotten
   away with one murder, he knows he can get away with
   another.

REMEMBERING DETAILS
2. How does Banquo plan to spend the afternoon before the
   banquet that night?
   (A) meeting with Ross and Lennox   (B) doing anything
   to get away from the castle   (C) riding with Fleance
   (D) none of the above.
3. It is clear from the things that the murderers say to
   Macbeth that
   (A) they will do anything   (B) Macbeth has talked them
   into committing murder for the first time   (C) they kill
   for a high price   (D) Macbeth has never seen either of
   them before.
4. After Macbeth convinces the murderers to kill Banquo,
   what else does he tell them to do?
   (A) leave the country immediately   (B) send him a message confirming that the job is done   (C) spread lies
   about who did it   (D) kill Fleance.

USING YOUR REASON
5. Macbeth complains that "For Banquo's issue I have filed
   my mind: For them the gracious Duncan have I
   murdered." By *them* he means
   (A) the murderers   (B) the witches   (C) Malcolm and
   Donalbain   (D) none of the above.

DRAWING CONCLUSIONS

6. Banquo says of Macbeth: "Thou has it now: King, Cawdor, Glamis, all, As the weird women promised, and I fear Thou play'dst most foully for 't." He is telling us
(A) that he fears that Macbeth has seen the witches again (B) that he wonders what title Macbeth will get next (C) that he suspects Macbeth is responsible for Duncan's murder   (D) that Macbeth may be playing a dangerous game.

7. Macbeth says of the witches: "Upon my head they placed a fruitless crown And put a barren scepter in my grip." He means that
(A) they made him a king with no sons to pass the title on to   (B) now that he feels so guilty, the symbols of kingship mean nothing to him   (C) he will rule over a very poor country   (D) none of the above.

THINKING IT OVER

In this scene what does Banquo seem to be most interested in?

Act III, Scene 2

FINDING THE MAIN IDEA

1. In this scene, Macbeth and Lady Macbeth admit to one another that
(A) they no longer love one another   (B) they must kill Banquo   (C) getting what they wanted has brought them misery   (D) nothing succeeds like success.

REMEMBERING DETAILS

2. What is Macbeth hiding from Lady Macbeth in this scene?
(A) his guilt and unhappiness   (B) his plans to have Banquo murdered   (C) his loss of appetite   (D) the dishes that will be served at that night's banquet.

DRAWING CONCLUSIONS

3. Lady Macbeth says to herself, before Macbeth comes in: "'Tis safer to be that which we destroy Than by destruction dwell in doubtful joy." She is saying
(A) in this world, it is better to destroy other people than have them destroy you (B) the next time we kill a person, we'll have somebody else do it (C) it is better to be the murder victim than the tormented murderer (D) it is safer to kill people the first time you think of it than to put off and worry about it.

USING YOUR REASON

4. Before Macbeth comes in, Lady Macbeth says something to herself that Macbeth repeats to her shortly after he comes in, indicating that they agree on one point. What is it?
(A) this marriage is making me miserable (B) it is clear that we have to stop killing people (C) the responsibilities of ruling Scotland are driving me crazy (D) it is better to be dead than to live in constant fear.

IDENTIFY THE MOOD

5. As this scene draws to an end, Macbeth says "Come, seeling night, Scarf up the tender eye of pitiful day, And with thy bloody and invisible hand Cancel and tear to pieces that great bond Which keeps me pale!" Macbeth is saying here
(A) that he is exhausted and looks forward to the night, when he can sleep (B) that he is waiting for night, which is the time that he prefers for Banquo's murder (C) that it has been a long day and he is looking forward to the banquet, where he can get away from Lady Macbeth (D) none of the above.

THINKING IT OVER

Why do you think that Macbeth does not want to tell Lady Macbeth about his plans to murder Banquo?

Act III, Scene 3

FINDING THE MAIN IDEA

1. What goes wrong with Macbeth's plans to murder Banquo?
   (A) a third murderer shows up (B) someone drops the torch (C) Banquo makes a lot of noise (D) Fleance gets away.

REMEMBERING DETAILS

2. How does the second murderer know in the dark that it is Banquo with the horses?
   (A) he recognizes Banquo's voice (B) either Banquo or Fleance is carrying a torch (C) all the other banquet guests have already arrived (D) none of the above

THINKING IT OVER

Why do you think Macbeth sent a third murderer without telling the first two murderers?

Act III, Scene 4

FINDING THE MAIN IDEA

1. It is not surprising that Macbeth's guilt feelings cause him to see Banquo's ghost, because
   (A) he never wanted to kill Banquo in the first place
   (B) he has had visions already in earlier scenes
   (C) the Scots have always believed in ghosts (D) it was time for some comic relief.

REMEMBERING DETAILS

2. After the guests leave, Macbeth notices that someone was missing from the banquet. Who was it?
   (A) Duncan (B) Malcolm (C) Banquo (D) none of the above
3. What evidence, other than the first murderer's story, does Macbeth have that the murder of Banquo has taken place?
   (A) a report from the third murderer (B) the appearance of Banquo's ghost (C) Banquo's absence from the banquet (D) blood on the first murderer's face.

DRAWING CONCLUSIONS

4. What does Macbeth mean when he says to himself, "There the grown serpent lies; the worm that's fled Hath nature that in time will venom breed, No teeth for th' present."

    (A) one snake down, one snake to go (B) kill a snake and another one takes its place (C) it was easy to kill Banquo, but now it will be almost impossible to kill Fleance (D) Banquo is dead, and Fleance, though he can cause no trouble now, will be dangerous in the future.

5. Macbeth says to Banquo's ghost "Never shake Thy gory locks at me." The ghost has gory locks because (A) Shakespeare wanted to frighten the audience (B) the first murderer told Macbeth about twenty gashes on Banquo's head (C) Macbeth has visions that involve blood (D) all of the above.

USING YOUR REASON

6. Judging from Lady Macbeth's comments while Macbeth is seeing Banquo's ghost, we can assume she is (A) depressed and withdrawn (B) angry and embarrassed (C) very concerned about Macbeth's mental health (D) as frightened as Macbeth.

7. By the end of the scene, Macbeth (A) is completely terrified (B) has decided that killing Banquo was not a good idea (C) is concerned that it is so late (D) seems to have recovered from the experience with the ghost.

THINKING IT OVER

Would you say that Macbeth's character has changed greatly in this scene?

Act III, Scene 5

FINDING THE MAIN IDEA

Hecate tells the witches to (A) stop fooling around and cause some real trouble for Macbeth (B) show more respect for witches' talents (C) give Macbeth a false sense of security (D) all of the above

Most Shakespeare experts believe that Shakespeare did not write this scene. It was probably put into the play after Shakespeare's retirement or death. Why do you think the scene was added?

Act III, Scene 6

FINDING THE MAIN IDEA

1. Why has Macduff gone to England?
(A) to escape from Macbeth (B) to ask King Edward of England to help Malcolm overthrow Macbeth (C) to establish his own claim to the throne (D) none of the above

REMEMBERING DETAILS

2. When Macbeth sent a messenger to England for Macduff,
(A) Macduff said very bad things to the messenger about Macbeth (B) Macduff said he had decided to become an English subject (C) Macduff refused to return to Scotland (D) Lennox helped Macduff hide from the messenger.

DRAWING CONCLUSIONS

3. The messenger from Macbeth tells Macduff, "You'll rue the time That clogs me with this answer." He is saying
(A) that Macduff should not have been so short (B) that Macduff will be sorry for giving him a message he does not want to take to Macbeth (B) that Macduff should not be so rude to servants (D) that Macduff should speak more openly about his feelings.

USING YOUR REASON

4. Why does Lennox think Macduff should "keep his distance" from Macbeth?
(A) he hopes Macduff will succeed in his efforts in England (B) he knows that Macbeth will have Macduff murdered if he can (C) he is unhappy over the state of affairs in Scotland (D) all of the above

THINKING IT OVER

In his opening speech in this scene, does Lennox mean everything he says? Explain.

Act IV, Scene 1

FINDING THE MAIN IDEA

1. During his second meeting with the witches, Macbeth believes that
(A) he has heard only good news (B) he has heard only bad news (C) he has heard both good and bad news
(D) none of the above.

REMEMBERING DETAILS

2. The first apparition tells Macbeth to
(A) stop asking so many questions (B) beware of Macduff (C) raise an army to fight Malcolm (D) return to Dunsinane.

3. The second apparition tells Macbeth that
(A) no human being can hurt him (B) he can be killed only by a supernatural being (C) no man born to a woman can harm him (D) he will live to a very old age.

4. The third apparition predicts that
(A) Macbeth will be defeated in the forest of Birnam
(B) when Macbeth is on Dunsinane hill, he will not be defeated (C) that he will not be defeated if he knows who is plotting against him (D) none of the above.

DRAWING CONCLUSIONS

5. When the witches show Macbeth a long line of kings who all look like Banquo, Macbeth says "Down! Thy crown does sear mine eyelids. And thy hair, Thou other gold-bound brow, is like the first." It is obvious
(A) the witches have given Macbeth what he wants (B) he is angry and upset (C) he fears another visit from Banquo's ghost (D) he is talking to Lennox.

263

6. Macbeth's comment "From this moment The very firstlings of my heart shall be The firstlings of my hand" tells us that from now on Macbeth
   (A) will know who his friends are and he will treat them accordingly (B) will call on the witches every time he need answers (C) will do what he needs to do quickly without worrying about whether he should or not (D) will not take Lennox along when he visits the witches.

USING YOUR REASON

7. We can assume from Macbeth's brief conversation with Lennox that
   (A) Lennox, like Banquo, saw the witches at the same time Macbeth did (B) Lennox has been spying on Macbeth (C) Lennox is plotting against Macduff and his family (D) none of the above.
8. Macbeth plans to wipe out Macduff's family
   (A) because the witches told him to (B) because Macduff has gone to England (C) because he hates other men whose names start with "Mac" (D) because the witches have confirmed his distrust of Macduff.

IDENTIFY THE MOOD

This is probably the best-known scene in Macbeth. It is not only important in the development of the story, but it has the magic and spectacle that all audiences like. The mood of fear and horror is increased by
(A) the disgusting ingredients of the witches' brew
(B) the apparition of the bloody child   (C) the thunder
(D) all of the above.

THINKING IT OVER

Do you think that the witches' appearance to Macbeth this time has had the effect on Macbeth that the witches wanted?

Act IV, Scene 2

FINDING THE MAIN IDEA

1. Lady Macduff and her oldest son die believing that
   (A) Macbeth had planned to kill them all along (B) if
   they had behaved politely, the murderers would have gone
   away (C) Macduff died before they did
   (D) Macduff has deserted them.

REMEMBERING DETAILS

2. Lady Macduff does not follow the messenger's advice to
   leave because
   (A) she is hoping that Macduff will return at any moment
   (B) she does not trust the messenger (C) she has done no
   one any harm (D) she does not want to live like a bird.

DRAWING CONCLUSIONS

3. When Ross tells Lady Macduff that Macduff is "noble,
   wise, judicious and best knows The fits o' th' season," he is
   (A) saying that she better forget all about Macduff
   (B) saying that Macduff knows how to protect himself
   (C) saying that Macduff cannot stand the bad weather in
   Scotland (D) saying that Macduff probably left for a
   good reason.

USING YOUR REASON

4. Ross is afraid that he will burst into tears because
   (A) he is afraid that Macduff is dead (B) he is as upset as
   Lady Macduff is over Macduff's leaving
   (C) he knows Lady Macduff is about to be murdered (D)
   none of the above.

5. Judging from his conversation with his mother, we could
   say that Macduff's son
   (A) cannot stop talking (B) is innocent but bright
   (C) is an annoying little brat (D) is interested only in
   birds.

THINKING IT OVER

If Macbeth had been in Macduff's castle and had
witnessed what happened in this scene, how would he
have felt?

Act IV, Scene 3

FINDING THE MAIN IDEA

1. Malcolm's greatest concern in his conversation with Macduff is
(A) why Macduff left his wife and children unprotected
(B) trying to find out who murdered his father (C) trying to find out if Macduff is on his side (D) none of the above.

2. The thing that both Malcolm and Macduff are most worried about is
(A) why Macduff left his wife and children unprotected
(B) the belief that King Edward can cure a disease
(C) the bad state of affairs in Scotland (D) none of the above.

3. We discover from the doctor
(A) that sickness is spreading all over England (B) that Edward is a king loved by his people (C) that real faith healers are almost never kings (D) that people will believe that kings can do anything.

4. When Macduff hears that his entire family has been murdered on Macbeth's orders
(A) he blames himself for their deaths (B) he plans to kill Macbeth's children (C) he decides to stay in England
(D) he takes it as a punishment from heaven.

REMEMBERING DETAILS

5. In order to test Macduff's loyalty, Malcolm describes himself as
(A) handsome, rich, and available (B) dangerous to know (C) oversexed, greedy, and criminal
(D) Scottish, stingy, and sly.

6. How does Macduff try to hide his grief when he hears that his family has been murdered?
(A) he runs from the scene (B) he laughs and tells jokes
(C) he weeps on Ross's shoulder (D) he pulls his hat over his face.

DRAWING CONCLUSIONS

7. What does Macduff mean when he says "O, I could play the woman with mine eyes"?
(A) I could weep (B) I am miserable (C) I could behave like a woman (D) all of the above.

8. When Malcolm says "Come, go we to the King. Our power is ready; Our lack is nothing but our leave," he is referring to
(A) King Macbeth (B) King Duncan (C) King Edward (D) King Malcolm.

USING YOUR REASON

9. Malcolm tells Macduff of the many faults in his own character and then reverses himself and says he will be perfect as king. After this conversation, Macduff
(A) takes the whole thing as a joke (B) is very angry with Malcolm (C) says that it is hard to know what to believe (D) knows that his family has been murdered.

THINKING IT OVER

Although there are many events in this scene, what is the most important overall theme?

Act V, Scene 1

FINDING THE MAIN IDEA

1. From what Lady Macbeth says when she is sleepwalking, we know that
(A) she cannot bear the guilt she feels for her part in the murders (B) she is not as tough as she thought she was (C) she regrets encouraging Macbeth to kill (D) all of the above.

REMEMBERING DETAILS

2. Until the doctor sees Lady Macbeth, the gentlewoman
(A) refuses to tell him about the sleepwalking (B) has no idea what is wrong with Lady Macbeth (C) has been sleepwalking herself (D) refuses to tell him what Lady Macbeth has been saying in her sleep.

267

DRAWING CONCLUSIONS

3. When Lady Macbeth asks, "Yet who would have thought the old man had so much blood in him?" who is she talking about?

   (A) the doctor (B) Duncan (C) Banquo (D) Macbeth

4. When Lady Macbeth says: "Wash your hands; put on your nightgown; look not so pale! I tell you yet again. Banquo's buried. He cannot come out on 's grave," she believes she is talking to

   (A) the doctor (B) the gentlewoman (C) Fleance
   (D) Macbeth.

THINKING IT OVER

Do the doctor and the gentlewoman know what Lady Macbeth is talking about? How do you know?

Act V, Scene 2

FINDING THE MAIN IDEA

1. We learn from the conversation among the four thanes that

   (A) Lady Macbeth has lost her mind (B) Macbeth's army is near Birnam Wood (C) Macbeth is losing his grip on Scotland (D) Donalbain will be joining Malcolm's army.

REMEMBERING DETAILS

2. Lennox tells Caithness that Donalbain
   (A) wants to be King of Scotland as well (B) will not be joining Malcolm in the battle (C) has sided with Macbeth (D) none of the above.

DRAWING CONCLUSIONS

3. Angus says of Macbeth, "Those he commands move only in command, Nothing in love." He means that
   (A) Macbeth is all business, and there's no time for play
   (B) There are plenty of commanders but no soldiers
   (C) Macbeth's men follow commands because they have to, not because they want to. (D) Macbeth has told his men to stay away from women.

Act V, Scene 3

FINDING THE MAIN IDEA

1. We learn in this scene that
(A) Malcolm's army is near   (B) someone has seen
Birnam Wood moving   (C) Lady Macbeth's condition is
getting better   (D) none of the above

REMEMBERING DETAILS

2. What is is that gives Macbeth courage in this scene?
(A) his belief in the words of the apparitions   (B) the
arming of the castle at Dunsinane   (C) the words of the
doctor   (D) Lady Macbeth's improving condition.

DRAWING CONCLUSIONS

3. The doctor says of Lady Macbeth's illness, "Therein the
patient Must minister to himself." He means that
(A) he cannot figure out what is bothering her   (B) he has
no treatment for guilty memories   (C) she could get
another doctor   (D) none of the above.

4. When Macbeth says "This push Will cheer me ever, or
disseat me now," he knows
(A) his life depends on Lady Macbeth's survival   (B) that
Seyton will bring bad news   (C) that the coming battle
will determine whether he rules or not   (D) that the battle
will mean life or death for him.

THINKING IT OVER

In this scene does Macbeth still believe that he will live
to a ripe old age?

Act V, Scene 4

FINDING THE MAIN IDEA

Malcolm tells his soldiers to carry branches from Birnam
Wood to Dunsinane to
(A) build forts for the battlefield   (B) conceal the
number of soldiers they have   (C) frighten Macbeth
(D) make the apparition's prediction come true.

Act V, Scene 5

FINDING THE MAIN IDEA
1. Macbeth's reaction to the death of Lady Macbeth
   (A) is about all one could expect from a bad king
   (B) shows that Macbeth no longer cares about her or anything   (C) shows that he should have listened to the doctor
   (D) has a great effect on the people who see it.
2. Macbeth decides to leave his castle and meet Malcolm in the field when he hears that
   (A) Lady Macbeth is dead   (B) Malcolm's army is smaller than expected   (C) his castle is no longer secure
   (D) none of the above.

REMEMBERING DETAILS
3. What is the first hint that Macbeth hears of Lady Macbeth's death?
   (A) a note from the doctor   (B) a word from the messenger
   (C) Seyton's announcement   (D) women screaming in the castle

DRAWING CONCLUSIONS
4. In his great speech in this scene, Macbeth says "Out, out, brief candle!" He is comparing a candle with
   (A) an actor   (B) fools   (C) idiots   (D) life
5. He also says "It is a tale Told by an idiot, full of sound and fury Signifying nothing." What is "It"?
   (A) the stage   (B) life   (C) the play   (D) yesterday

USING YOUR REASON
6. When Macbeth says "I 'gin to be aweary of the sun, And wish th'estate o' th' world were now undone," he is
   (A) longing for night again   (B) looking forward to death
   (C) hoping for the end of the world   (D) all of the above

THINKING IT OVER
Is Macbeth surprised by the turn of events in this scene?

Act V, Scene 6

When Malcolm addresses his commanders this time
(A) he is calling for more sneaky moves (B) he is calling for all-out war (C) he is wondering where Macduff is (D) none of the above.

Act V, Scene 7

1. As a result of Young Siward's death, Macbeth assumes that
   A) Macduff is nowhere to be found (B) one prediction of the apparitions is true (C) Young Siward is not brave enough (D) the battle has reached a turning point.

REMEMBERGING DETAILS

2. Macduff enters
   (A) looking for Young Siward (B) slightly wounded (C) looking for Macbeth (D) looking for Malcolm.
3. We know from the brief conversation between Siward and Malcolm that
   (A) they know of Young Siward's death (B) Macbeth's castle has been captured (C) Macbeth's men are winning (D) Macbeth's men cannot see what they are doing.

Act V, Scene 8

1. Macbeth discovers in this scene that
   (A) Macduff is a supernatural being (B) that Malcolm has already been named King of Scotland (C) that he has been tricked by the powers of darkness (D) that he has been blamed for the death of Young Siward.

REMEMBERING DETAILS

2. What is Macbeth thinking about when the scene opens?
   (A) Lady Macbeth (B) the upcoming fight with Macduff (C) holding onto his throne (D) suicide

3. Macbeth decides to fight Macduff because
(A) he does not believe Macduff's story about not being born (B) Macduff gives him no choice (C) Macduff threatens to exhibit Macbeth like a freak (D) he is better armed than Macduff.

DRAWING CONCLUSIONS

4. When Macduff tells Macbeth of his unusual birth, Macbeth says "And be these juggling fiends no more believed, That palter with us in a double sense." What does he mean by "juggling"?
(A) wiggling (B) from a circus (C) tricky (D) drunk
5. Macbeth's last words are "Lay on, Macduff; And damned be him that first cries 'Hold, enough!'" He means
(A) that whoever gives up will go to hell (B) Watch out!
(C) that he does not believe Macduff's statement about his birth (D) that whoever gives up will be killed and go to hell.

USING YOUR REASON

6. We can see from Macbeth's statement "Though Birnam Wood be come to Dunsinane, And thou opposed, being of no woman born, Yet I will try the last" that
(A) Macbeth's evil is endless (B) Macbeth is glad not to have to commit suicide (C) Macbeth has a final moment of his old bravery (D) none of the above
7. Macbeth's statement when Macduff first challenges him is "Of all men else I have avoided thee. But get thee back! My soul is too much charged With blood of thine already." There is the possibility here that
(A) Macbeth knows he cannot beat Macduff
(B) Macbeth may have some guilt feelings left
(C) he already knows Macduff was not born to a woman
(D) none of the above.
8. Judging by his final speech, we can assume that Malcolm
(A) thinks Lady Macbeth killed herself (B) is eager to please everyone there (C) is already behaving like a king (D) all of the above.

9. Siward feels that his son died
(A) unnecessarily (B) violently (C) bravely (D) none of the above

THINKING IT OVER

Do you think Macbeth has any admirable qualities left in this scene?